I0589483

Potions
and
Paper Cranes

Lan Fang
Translated from the Indonesian by
Elisabet Titik Murtisari

Potions
and
Paper Cranes

TRANSLATOR'S NOTE

Getting this project was beyond my wildest imagination. Having worked in the field of translation for more than fifteen years, I know far too well I can only translate with skill into Indonesian, my mother tongue. However, the motivation to support Indonesian literature claim the place it deserves on the stage of world literature with a voice of its own, and the support of two editors, I signed the contract. After a very sleepless night, I embarked on the journey of translating *Perempuan Kembang Jepun* into *Potions and Paper Cranes.*

Narrated from different points of view by each character, *Potions and Paper Cranes* explores the individual psyches and struggles of the protagonists, as well as antagonists, with poverty, desire, and survival. Repetition is sometimes inevitable but this helps bring to light the broken lives of its personae: Lestari/Kaguya, Tjoa Kim Hwa/Matsumi, Sujono, and Sulis. At the end of the story, the reader is invited not to judge or demonize any character, but to accept everyone's pain and wounds as irrevocable parts of life.

In translating *Potions and Paper Cranes* I have tried to be faithful to the source text, and in doing so I have learned the importance of the editor's role in any given publication. The historical and cultural elements are strong features of the novel. Therefore, I have painstakingly researched the material. Growing up with my brother's two big historical photography books on hand, the history of Indonesian independence is particularly close to my heart. This provided a strong foundation in checking the details of my country's past. In order to render the material accurately, at times I had to modify the original text.

My traditional Javanese background has been resourceful in assuring an accurate rendering of cultural details in the story. My adventurous wanderings as a child (without my mother's permission) in nearby *kampungs* (native villages) and a former Dutch army barrack helped me greatly in understanding the kampung setting that often appears in the novel, and prompted the change of plywood to bamboo as the material used as the room divider in Sulis's grandmother's tiny room.

I am blessed with the multicultural environment of my city, Salatiga, which helped me relate to the Chinese diaspora culture in the novel. *Potions and Paper Cranes* offers an excellent snapshot of Indonesia's Chinese cultural aspect and its history, which helped build a substantial portion of Indonesia's economy.

It was through these encounters, and from the elements of life I share with Lan Fang, that I developed strong ownership of the project and felt empowered to retell the story of *Potions and Paper Cranes* in English.

A special thanks goes to Ari for sharing about Japanese culture, and Tyas and Marina for the support of friendship.

Elisabet Titik Murtisari
July 2013

Lan Fang is indebted to:

Time
The owner of the past, present, and future

Bapak Budi Darma
I'm at a loss for words!

Bapak Johan—Togamas Bookstore
and Father Sindhunata
Always and always…

Bapak Dukut Imam Widodo and Bapak Suparta Brata
Very supportive resources

Mas Bambang AW—artist,
Mas Peter Wang—photographer
Sin Lan Bridal and Salon
Sonny Radji—fashion designer
Made this novel lively

Mas Akmal NB, Mbak Endah Perca, Mas Hermawan Aksan
Mas Hernadi Tanzil, Mas Kurnia Effendi, Ibu Senny
Alwasilah, Mas Veven Sp Wardhana
Extraordinary chemistry came so naturally
Unbelievable!

Bu Lis
Mbak Anas, Hetih, Mbak Ike, Indah, Iwan, Vera
Amazing teamwork!

The readers
Enjoy it

Potions
and
Paper Cranes

Prologue

Surabaya, October 2003

Lestari took down a set of cups from the cupboard. Today a special guest was coming to visit the orphanage. This was not someone interested in adopting a child or giving a donation, but a truly special guest.

Lestari ran an orphanage in Surabaya—or more appropriately a shelter for abandoned babies and children. She had never put up a sign.

She looked after the modest house where she and her late father used to live, and now used as a shelter. At the beginning, she only took care of one or two babies to get rid of her loneliness, since she only had her father. But as time passed, more babies stayed at the shelter, entrusted to her or simply abandoned. Some were disabled and it was not clear where they came from as their parents had forsaken them. Occasionally a young pregnant woman without a man willing to marry her arrived at the shelter. The woman usually stayed until she gave birth, and then left the baby with Lestari. Every month more babies came and filled the house with their cries and babbles.

Thank God, the more babies arrived, the more couples came to adopt them. Day by day babies were born. Babies were adopted. Those babies came and went.

Lestari managed the orphanage with administration fees from adopting couples and donations. She did not charge a certain rate to couples that wanted to adopt. Instead, she asked about their origin and reasons for adopting because she wanted to make sure the babies had loving parents. Couples who adopted from Lestari frequently became permanent donors, and their donations provided for other orphans.

She was sixty years old and unmarried. Her age had not erased her past beauty from her face. A pair of thick eyebrows framed her beautiful round eyes behind curled eyelashes. She had smooth, fair, olive skin, a pointed nose, and sensuous lips. She spoke with polite, gentle words and her motherly voice was soft and melodious. Many people were curious why she was not, or more precisely, did not want to get married. With her beauty, it was impossible that no man had ever approached her. The deep, long scars on her cheeks that looked like scratches did not diminish the beauty of her youth.

What made her unattractive was the cold and somber expression in her eyes. They were cold as ice, and somber as dusk. Her beautiful face always looked as gloomy as a cloudy sky. Her lips hardly ever curved into a smile, and if she did smile, it was just a polite expression because her eyes remained empty.

*****

Lestari had an adopted daughter named Maya, a child left at the orphanage by a beggar.

Last week, the girl announced with sparkling eyes, "Mom, Higashi's coming soon."

"And…?" Lestari glanced at Maya.

"He's bringing his mother."

"So?"

"Oh, Mom. Don't you have anything else to say?" the girl pouted.

Lestari faintly smiled when she noticed Maya sulking. "So what should I do? Grandpa died not even one hundred days ago. I've neglected a lot of my work during the last six months when Grandpa was sick. There's the babies, the nurses, the guests, the administration…" She did not finish her sentence and took a deep breath. Her smile was suddenly gone and her gloomy expression had returned.

Lestari rested her eyes on the paper birds hanging on the left side of her desk. Whenever he had spare time, her father made those paper cranes from the colorful origami paper she regularly bought for him.

Her father liked to sit in his wheelchair by the window. He liked to watch the morning sun climb high and paint white clouds in the blue sky. He also liked to watch the evening sun set with beams of golden orange. He really loved the sun, she thought. He almost never passed a single day without enjoying the sunrise and sunset. Those old wrinkled eyes always looked at the sun with a mysterious gaze. Sometimes they seemed to be filled with a memory of love.

Love? She did not dare to find out about it, because she also saw deep emptiness, long loneliness, and recurring pain.

During such times, her father would sigh deeply, light his cigarette, inhale deeply, and cough until he gasped for air.

"Dad, the doctor said you shouldn't smoke," Lestari always reminded him.

He didn't seem to hear. Another puff of his cigarette caused another coughing spasm. After he calmed down, his wrinkled hands would grab a stack of origami paper, which she kept near him, and fold the sheets one by one into cranes. When they piled up, he threaded most of them into a long strand and arranged the rest nicely on the table. His parched thin lips then broke into a smile.

"This is called origami, the Japanese art of paper folding. And those paper cranes are *orisurus*," he rasped, as if talking to a shadow he could only see in his mind. He always liked watching the sun and making orisurus.

There was a time when he looked after the small garden he had planted next to the orphanage, talked to Maya, or just walked around to check on the babies in their cribs. But since his stroke five years ago, he became paralyzed and had trouble speaking. He seemed to have lost his zest for living and spent his days in the wheelchair, watching the sun and making orisurus. The situation worsened after the doctor told him he had stage IV lung cancer and predicted he would not live more than six months. The cancer gnawed on half of his lungs and spread to his throat and vocal cords.

"Matsumi taught me origami," her father once told Lestari when she asked him who had shown him how to make the paper birds.

"Matsumi?" Lestari frowned as she fed him a spoonful of porridge. This was done slowly and carefully to keep him from choking, and so the porridge would not fill the small breathing tube in his throat.

"Did you like Matsumi?" she asked him.

The old man ran the tip of his tongue across his thin dry lips. She could see his teeth, blackened by the cigarettes that had given him lung cancer.

"Very much. Loved her very much," he mumbled.

Lestari knew what was in his eyes. It was more than love, hurt, emptiness, or loneliness. She saw love embedded in pain, or was it pain embedded in love? She sensed a wounded love, a lonely, hollow love. What did that mean? Was it yearning? Was it longing?

Lestari heaved a long sigh. Her father was eighty-five and she was sixty. Where and when did he meet Matsumi? Why did he miss her? Who was she? What was she like?

Was she like the sun?

Or the origami birds?

"Matsumi came from *Amaterasu Omikami*—the sun goddess—and she went back to her. She was like an origami bird that flew away and disappeared. What is left are only memories…" He struggled to finish his sentence. A rivulet of clear water ran along his dark, wrinkled cheeks. He tried to reach for them but his hand could not move.

Lestari wiped her father's cheeks with the back of her hand.

She gave another long sigh.

Every time she looked at her father, tears filled her eyes. The doctor had inserted the tube in his throat to help him breathe. She sterilized the breathing tube every morning and afternoon, and helped him eat, drink, and take his medicine.

She did everything for her father. He had done everything for her decades ago, when he bathed and fed her and combed her hair. He tried to make her talk when she was sad and did not feel like talking anymore.

Memories of him flickered in Lestari's mind. Her father's love had been so great, he was present in every particle of the past she was unable to banish from her mind. Lestari had few memories about her father she could recall without pain. In order to keep the good from mixing with the bad, Lestari built two imaginary boxes. The small one about her father's love was always open; the other and much larger one was kept shut and hidden in the farthest corner of her soul.

Whenever Lestari saw her father, she felt she was very much like him. They both loved the sun, and spent hours watching the rise and set without uttering a word.

Although she never spoke about it, she remembered how she spent her childhood sitting quietly on the doorstep waiting for her father to come home from work while watching the sunset.

When he finally came, he would stroke her head and ask, "Has it been a long time since the sun set?"

Lestari would nod. The sun always set a long time before he came home. The sky was already dark, but she'd be outside counting the stars and waiting for her father to hold her hand and talk to her. Though she rarely responded to anything he said, he talked about everything: his job at the harbor, the little candy marbles he bought for her, the dark coffee gone cold after its steam evaporated, and even the buzzing mosquitoes.

That was how she spent her years until she grew up and became an adult.

He grew old, too.

As time passed, she was no longer a child and he was no longer a muscular man—she became an adult woman and he an aged man in a wheelchair.

She took care of him, feeding, preparing medications, and talking to him. He was an old man who sat in his wheelchair and stared at the sun without saying a word.

The only thing that did not change was their love of the sun.

After Lestari finished serving him, she often saw her father look at her with love. His eyes glistened as he held back tears, and tried to utter with his nasal raspy voice, "Thank you. You are beautiful like your mother."

"Beautiful?" she mumbled with pain.

The word "beautiful" was in the large box she did not want to open. She was scared of opening it and finding the word inside. She never felt beautiful. She only knew pain.

What about the word "mother"?

Mother? For the hundredth time the word opened a wound in her heart, making it bleed and fester.

She had never said the word since her father asked her to leave the woman she called Mother. With tears in her eyes, Lestari remembered the woman who caused the chaos in her life and had carved the scars on her face and in her heart.

During the two months before his death, her father mentioned Matsumi more often. He always said her name with much affection, but could not talk about her because of his weakening condition. He only muttered that name and left a pile of origami birds. Although Lestari really wanted to know more about her, she believed Matsumi was a mystery she could not unravel.

"Mom." Maya interrupted Lestari's daydreaming.

"Yes?" she turned her eyes from the origami birds.

"We don't need to make a big welcome party for Higashi although his mother will be with him. He said he just wants to introduce us." Maya continued talking about Higashi's visit.

Lestari said softly, "What's making you so nervous, excited, and happy? Is it because of Higashi or meeting his mother?"

"Both, Mom," Maya answered quickly. "Of course, seeing Higashi again makes me happy, but this time he's with his mother. You know he is an orphan, right? She was the woman who adopted him. So we can say she is his parent, Mom."

Lestari remembered when Maya first introduced Higashi to her. When she asked where he was from, she never thought he was an orphan.

"My foster mother runs a *ryokan,* a traditional inn in Kyoto. She adopted me when I was five days old. The woman who gave birth to me was too young to be a mother. She was only sixteen and worked as a maid in a small shop next to the gallery. My biological father did not have a job and left my mother. I have never met them."

Lestari could not say anything after hearing Higashi's story. A deep sadness crept in her veins. They shared the same absence since she had never known her mother.

Her father, although loving her very much, had kept the secret about her mother.

Lestari could feel Higashi's misery. Maya had also been abandoned. Many babies in the orphanage had the same fate as Higashi and Maya. They were like the tips of pens dancing on the same black piece of paper. Only good fortune could change the color of the paper to grey, but never to white. The dark footsteps always lingered. For them, life was like a dice on the gaming table.

"My adopted mother was very old when she took me in. I am more suitable to be her grandson, and she really loves me. She raised and educated me until I graduated from university. I have liked drawing since I was a child. Besides studying at university, I learned to draw. My paintings sold pretty well so I could finally have my own gallery. Well, it's only a small gallery, but it's not bad."

Lestari did not want Maya to have a relationship with a foreigner. Even worse, he was Japanese. God knows why, but Japan was like a nightmare haunting her. Was it because of her father, or Matsumi, the name her father often mentioned? But Higashi's modesty touched her. She could see honesty, a hard-working spirit, responsibility, and devotion in him. He spoke in an orderly, calm, and polite manner and his black eyes reflected intelligence and determination. He was tall, with fair skin like that of a typical Japanese. She had to admit he was an attractive young man.

Lestari knew her dislike of Japan was unfair to Maya. The country was a dark shroud wrapped around her father, and this made her distrust Higashi. Maya did not know anything about the shroud. Maya had nothing to do with Japan. If she had a relationship with a Japanese man, it was not done to tear open Lestari's old wound.

"Oh, I see." Lestari quickly diverted her thoughts. "Higashi will introduce you to his mother, won't he?" Lestari watched Maya blush. She liked teasing her daughter.

How quickly time passed. When she met Maya for the first time, she was just a snotty, filthy child, but now she had metamorphosed into an attractive young woman. Like in a fairy tale, the ugly duckling had turned into a beautiful swan.

She still remembered when a shabby woman stood at her door holding the hand of a three-year-old girl. The girl wore ragged clothes and no slippers, her dark face was covered with dirt, and her hand wiped at the mucus running from her nose. Lestari had often seen the woman begging by the lamppost on the street corner in front of the orphanage.

One day the woman came and entrusted her with the little girl. She said she was going home to her village in the country for two or three days. She said that when she returned she'd pick up the girl she claimed to be her daughter.

A week passed and the woman did not return, and the girl she left never cried looking for her. Once Lestari asked the little girl if the woman was her mother. The child shook her head while enjoying the cookies in her hands. Lestari also asked where she came from, where her mother lived, and her name. The three-year-old girl only smiled, her clear eyes indicating that she did not understand a thing Lestari had said. Her innocent smile and clear eyes made Lestari fall in love with her.

"What if I was your mother? Would you like that?" Lestari asked.

The girl grinned while spreading her arms and reaching out to her. Lestari took the child in her arms. When the girl laid her head on her chest, Lestari felt something warm surge inside her heart. "What if I named you Maya? Your past is illusory, an unreal shadow you don't need to remember. Your future is now with me."

Since that day, Maya was her "daughter."

When Lestari told her father she had adopted the girl, he agreed. Stroking Maya's cheek, he said "Lestari, you were about her age when…" Like usual, he did not finish his sentence.

Her father loved Maya, and so did everyone else at the orphanage. Maya was a loveable little girl—she was cheerful and her babbling made people laugh. Her presence filled the loneliness always in the hearts of Lestari and her father.

Maya had grown into a lovely girl. No one would have thought she was once a street child who came to the orphanage in rags. No one could see that she was a child without a clear parentage. She had turned into a smart, beautiful, cheerful, and confident woman.

Maya finished her studies in Japanese literature and worked at the Japanese cultural center in Surabaya. Last year she introduced Higashi to Lestari.

Higashi came to Surabaya to cover Kembang Jepun, the city's largest trade center, also known as the city's Chinatown. It was not clear where the name came from. People said that a very attractive Japanese woman used to live there, so it was called Kembang Jepun, which means "the Japanese flower."

After the Dutch and Japanese occupations, the area became known as a trade center. The many Chinese residents opened shops, restaurants, and also glitzy nightclubs with gorgeous women. Higashi said Surabaya with its Kembang Jepun was very famous in Japan. Even his mother knew about it.

"My mother used to live in Surabaya for some time. She said she once stayed in Kembang Jepun. When she was young, she was really enchanting."

Lestari suddenly felt a headache after hearing what Higashi had said. She did not know why, but the story made her uncomfortable. Something tore at her heart, an old wound she never understood but always cast a shadow in her dreams.

Maya met Higashi when he visited her office for information about Kembang Jepun. He came around the time of the Surabaya Art Festival to celebrate the city's anniversary. Kembang Jepun had changed much since the Japanese occupation, and was now one of the most festive public spaces for the anniversary celebration.

Higashi was stunned when Maya told him the neighborhood was no longer known for its nightclubs, but had turned into the economic artery of Surabaya. Still, its cultural heritage had not faded.

Since then, Maya and Higashi were close. She often accompanied him as he took photographs of life at Kembang Jepun, which he later painted on canvas.

Kembang Jepun was crowded in the afternoon, with sounds of Surabaya Chinese dialect mixed with various Madurese accents. The old buildings and shops, relics of the Dutch and Japanese occupations, were yet to be displaced by modern office buildings. The quick heartbeat of Kembang Jepun manifested in the passing vans, pickups, cars, trucks, and even pedicabs. The pungent breath of Chinatown was apparent from Kembang Jepun to Jembatan Merah, the

Red Bridge, through the fragrance of incense from the old temples on Dukuh and Slompretan Street and the body odor of male and female Madurese laborers blending with the aromas of garlic, shallots, spices, and salted fish at the Pabean Market.

Kembang Jepun was just as lively in the evening. At the mouth of Kembang Jepun near Jembatan Merah stood a Chinese gate with two pairs of huge high pillars. On top of the gate, two writhing Chinese dragons raised their snouts and played with a golden fireball. A pair of marble lion statues stood at each side like gatekeepers. Street pillars were adorned with the twelve animals of the Chinese zodiac and connected by arches hung with hundreds of exotic red lampions. These illuminated the whole street and turned the dark sky into bright red.

In the evening, after the trading at Kembang Jepun had stopped, the area turned into a food and pedestrian center with an oriental atmosphere. The tantalizing aromas from the food stalls along the road invited people to sit, drink, eat, chat, and laugh in relaxed surroundings and rid themselves of the fatigue from the day's work.

Kembang Jepun also became the main road for the city's annual cultural festivals. The performance of the quick and lively movements of the Chinese lion dance along with the dynamic Javanese *Reog Ponorogo* was not an unusual sight. The people watching along the road applauded and often threw money into the lion's mouth and reog head.

"It's a big mistake if you're looking for nightclubs in Kembang Jepun. You will not find them," Maya said laughing.

"The Kembang Jepun I see is very different from what my mother told me," Higashi said to Maya. "This one is so exotic, so dynamic."

"During the Dutch colonization, the road was called Handel Straat. No one knows how it later turned into Kembang Jepun or who gave it that name, maybe because there were many Jepun flowers. Indonesians used to call Japan 'Jepun.' There were many glamorous girls here," Maya said smiling.

"My mother lived in Kembang Jepun for quite some time. She worked in a big Chinese restaurant. She was beautiful, indeed. Although she is old, the beauty of her youth still shines through. She cannot forget this place. She said she fell in love as well as suffered here. If I'm not mistaken, she left a daughter here before returning to Japan."

"Really?" Maya was surprised. "Where is the daughter now?"

"I don't know. After Indonesia won its independence and Japan recovered from its economic collapse, she looked for her in Surabaya several times, but did not find her."

When Higashi returned to Kyoto, he stayed in contact with Maya by email. Maya said his paintings that portrayed Kembang Jepun sold well in Kyoto. Japanese people thought they were exotic. Even Higashi's mother was impressed. She said Kembang Jepun had changed a lot.

Today, Higashi would visit Lestari's orphanage with his adoptive mother. Thinking she was a Japanese woman who had lived in Kembang Jepun made Lestari nervous.

Maya interrupted her reverie. "Mom, Higashi and his mother are waiting in the office."

Lestari took a deep breath to calm her trembling heart. She did not understand why she was overcome with such anxiety.

She walked to her office while trying hard to calm herself. When she reached the threshold, she saw Higashi sitting with his back to the door. A woman of medium height with neatly combed silver hair looked at the pile of origami birds on the table. Although she was old, she still looked healthy and fit.

"Good morning," Lestari greeted them with a voice that sounded strange to her own ears. Her heart pounded faster.

Higashi rose and turned his head. His adoptive mother also turned her head.

The old woman's eyes pierced Lestari, and she felt something warm stream through her heart. Stunned, she tried to remember when it was the last time she felt such a sensation. It had been a long time, but when? Lestari desperately tried to remember.

"*Ohayo gozaimasu,* good morning." The old woman's voice sounded like it came from another world. It was soothing, soft, and cool. It rung in Lesari's ears and threw her back to a time that was only dark.

When was it? Where was it?

Driven by an unknown strength, Lestari bowed in respect to the old woman. She knew that was what Japanese did when they were introduced. They did not just shake hands.

"*Okasan, kochira no kata wa* Maya-*san no okasan desu.* Mother, this is Maya's mother," Higashi said.

She bowed once more. "Lestari," she said.

The woman greeted her with a soft voice. "Lestari-san?"

"Yes. My name is Lestari," she replied slowly.

"Lestari-san loves origami?" the old woman asked her in Indonesian. She turned to the scattered paper birds on the table.

Lestari lifted her head. "My father made them," she answered.

"Father?" Higashi's adoptive mother asked. "This is origami. Was your father Japanese?"

"No, he wasn't," Lestari answered. "My father was Javanese. He learned origami from a Japanese woman when he was young. Her name was Matsumi."

The old woman appeared perplexed. Her peaceful eyes turned uneasy. She looked closely at Lestari.

"Where does he live?" Her voice was tense.

"My father passed away three months ago."

"Passed away?" she exclaimed.

"Yes, he passed away," Lestari repeated.

"What is your name?" The woman's deep voice trembled.

"Lestari."

"Only Lestari?" The tone of her raised voice indicated her doubting Lestari's response.

"Yes, that's what my father called me."

"What was his name?" the old woman interrupted her again.

"Sujono."

The old woman's face turned pale as death before she said, "I'm Matsumi."

Lestari felt as if she had been struck by lightning. The earth beneath her feet spun ten times faster.

Part 1: Sulis

Surabaya, 1941–1942

His passion was wild.

I looked at the door, restlessly. The hands of the alarm clock Grandma had given me showed eleven, but *Mas* Sujono—my husband—was still not home. True, he often came home very late at night, sometimes as late as two in the morning.

He often reeked of alcohol and, being drunk, his dark face looked like red copper. Sometimes he muttered nonsense before he vomited and let the foul smell fill our tiny room.

When he came home drunk, I would collect the bucket, mop, and eucalyptus oil. I took off his clothes drenched in sweat and vomit. While he lay on his back, I first washed his body, and then massaged his chest with eucalyptus oil. Soon afterward he'd fall asleep, snoring contently.

I hardly do that anymore. I don't have the slightest intention to take care of him. He can be sick without a massage and sleep in his clothes soiled with sweat and rice wine vomit.

I don't have any feelings left for Mas Sujono and hate being trapped in a life with him. Yes, I really feel trapped, and hate him more and more everyday.

I do not care if he comes home drunk. I just felt obliged to open the door rather than let him bang on it and disturb the neighbors. I am not obligated to wash and take care of his dirty and sweaty body. Doing the daily chores like washing the clothes, cooking, making coffee, and serving him on the sleeping mat was more than enough for what he gave me: a meager sum of money for daily needs, a gabby mouth, and violence.

I often looked at his face under the dim lantern's light and wondered how I got trapped in a wrong marriage with that man.

Wrong marriage or wrong man, I argued with myself.

Mas Sujono was tall and thin. He had narrow sloping shoulders, a thin chest, deep-set eyes, a pointed nose, and very thin lips.

The Javanese say thin lips fit a woman better. Her face looks prettier with such lips—they make her look flirty, especially when she purses her lips or pouts. They also say such a woman is more talkative and attractive, but what if a man has such lips?

Mas Sujono's lips were thin, and he was a blabbermouth. He always talked about this country, his broken dream, his hatred of the Dutch, our poverty, and also Joko, our son.

Soekarno and Hatta were his idols. He wanted to be a soldier and join the fight for independence, but he could not do this because I did not want him to join the resistance. Honestly, I do not have strong feelings of nationalism and patriotism. I would rather think about my own life and little child than the country, which is always chaotic with bombings and whizzing bullets. I was afraid that I might become a young widow while still needing to raise our child. I did not care if it gave me the title of "independence fighter's widow," or "hero's widow," or whatever. What I wanted was for my son and me to survive in this difficult country.

Mas Sujono missed finishing high school so he could not work at an office. The only native people who did came from certain social groups, especially the *priyayis* and Indonesian Chinese with enough education. Besides, Mas Sujono hated the Dutch and did not want to work for them.

He always said, "The Dutch are bastards. The Chinese are stingy but they are only merchants. They do not oppress people like the Dutch."

Mas Sujono had a high sense of nationalism. He said the Dutch exploited our country's wealth and caused Indonesians to be lazy. They colonized us for hundreds of years and gave us only poverty and suffering.

"This country must be independent to prosper. The people should feed their own stomachs, not those of the mad Dutch," he said with curses.

I did not care. Millions of people were very poor in this messed-up country, and had to work as forced laborers to build roads and railroad tracks. They suffered starvation because of the poverty the Dutch created, and had to fight to feed their own stomachs.

So did I and I was more worried about what we would eat the next day than this country's freedom. My life was difficult enough—independence was not my business.

Mas Sujono did not care about his family. He preferred to be a war commentator of the news he heard on a neighbor's radio while smoking his rolled cigarette, or stay out with his friends playing dominos while getting drunk. He never held a steady job or worked at the same place for more than two months. Meanwhile I had to look after my son. As everyone had to eat, we had more fights over our shortage of money.

Mas Sujono thought I never stopped harassing him. He said I asked too much and demanded far beyond what he could afford. Was I wrong to ask for money to feed our son?

Our son, or my son?

Mas Sujono said Joko was not his flesh and blood. He berated me for being already pregnant when we married. He did not believe the child in my womb was his. It was Mas Wandi's, he insisted.

I knew Mas Wandi before Sujono. He drove a pedicab for a living and would often stop at Tanjung Perak, the seaport, to get passengers. He was forty-two. Even though almost my father's age, his body was still robust with a muscular chest, back, and arms. Sometimes his sweat made his muscles look shiny under the sun, and his body odor blended with the scent of the sun and the tobacco of his hand-rolled cigarettes. Secretly I enjoyed this aroma when he sat near me.

Tanjung Perak had only a handful of pedicabs. People still used trams and bicycles, and many scrambled for the pedicabs soon after a ship docked at the port. Most of the ship's passengers were Chinese who had just arrived in Surabaya. God knows why so many yellow-skinned and slant-eyed people came to the city. People said they left their country because the Japanese had destroyed it, and also the communist rebellion.

I knew nothing of what was happening. I only saw very tired faces when the Chinese entered Surabaya. This might have been caused by the months at sea, or the war that had wrecked their country.

Indonesia was not much different. Wherever I looked, all I saw were sad faces.

I was often at the port of Tanjung Perak, where I went to sell *jamu*. Many customers bought my potions and Mas Wandi was the most generous. He always paid more for the one *batok,* or half coconut shell, of jamu he bought. He never asked for the change. Instead, he often secretly stuck a banknote in my bra while fondling my breasts.

I was shocked the first time he slipped me some money and grabbed my breasts, but his touch also made me shiver. Mas Wandi was the first man who touched me. Not knowing what to do, I was quiet. I was embarrassed and nervous, but unable to hold off the strange sensations. I enjoyed his touch, and didn't do anything about it.

Such incidents happened frequently among jamu peddlers. It was quite common to take one of us to a plain room in the nearby brothels along East and West Kalimas Street. Since Tanjung Perak turned into a commercial port, such enterprises had grown.

At first, I offered my jamu to the women who lived in the dim light of the brothel rooms' lanterns, women who were awake at night and slept during the day. The potions in the bottles I carried in my basket were all meant for women: potions for a tired body and old pregnancy, sweet rice and ginger potion, betel leaf potion to tighten the woman-ness, slimming potion, and tamarind leaf refreshing potion.

But as time went by, I sold my jamu not only to women but also the men who enjoyed the warmth of their bodies— men who went in and out of their tiny rooms. Most of them were seaport coolies who normally sat at the eatery shops, which also served as brothels. They liked to sip *legen*, a sweet beverage made of palm sap, while smoking a hand-rolled *klobot* cigarette with a very sharp, pungent smell. Their shoulders and backs were dirty with hemp dust from the gunnysacks they used to protect their skin from the goods they lifted.

When evening fell and dusk started to crawl in, the women came out of their rooms and showed their cleavage. They chanted *parikan* poetry, flirty and inviting:

Tanjung Perak, Mas
The captain's found a treasure.
Please, come here, Mas
My room is full of pleasure.
They continued one another's parikan with giggles. Rice wine flowed when the night came, not only warming the spirits but also heating the flesh. The women rubbed their bulging breasts against the men's sweaty brawny backs, inviting strong hands to slip money into their bras. They wrapped their arms around the men and walked through the dancing shadows of the dim lantern's light to a room.

Moans, groans, wetness, and sweat.

I met Mas Wandi in one of the brothels. A virgin never touched by a man, I was awkward, shy, and embarrassed. When he touched my bosom, his hand felt hot and caused a wave of pleasure. After a while, I craved it. I did not stay passive or feel nervous and shy anymore. I became more daring, and I did not hesitate to get closer to him when I wanted him to squeeze my breasts.

Mas Wandi knew what I wanted.

"You're so tempting, little girl," he said, while fondling me.

Soon the quick touches were not enough. As a girl growing into a woman, I felt a burning passion that demanded more, and even more. I wanted to do what the women and men did in those dim tiny rooms. I wanted to feel his hands touch all of my breasts. So I held his hands to keep him longer.

"Seriously. Especially this part," he said while gazing at me and giving my breast another squeeze.

I felt aroused when his breath blew against my ear and down my neck.

"Really? *Yu* Ning is prettier than me, and Yu Sih even more so," I replied sulkily.

"They don't attract me," he whispered passionately in my ear.

Was I flirting? Had I tempted and seduced him?

I don't know.

I liked him. He always gave me extra money for face powder and lip color, and I liked his squeezes, too.

Yu Ning and Yu Sih, who were jamu peddlers like me, often said sleeping with a man makes you quiver.

The women were three and four years older than me. Yu Ning had dim, melancholic eyes but she was hot and fiery on the sleeping mat, or so I heard from the men who talked about her. Yu Sih had a round gentle-looking Javanese face with fair olive skin. Many men wanted to see more of her smooth body.

I was not that pretty and well aware of it. The sun had darkened my skin, and my hands were big and coarse. My heels were also cracked. My face is not oval like Yu Sih, but square and strong-jawed, and my eyes are big and wide, not dim and melancholic like Yu Ning. I often cursed my face because I could not attract as many customers as Yu Ning and Yu Sih.

"They are nothing compared to you, little girl. Look at your body. Men who are not attracted to it can't be real men," Mas Wandi said.

While I was only sixteen, my body was fully developed. I had a big, full, round bust, hips, and bottom. My breasts had big nipples, and were firm and bouncy when I touched them. They made my *kebaya* look very tight and almost bulge out. My rounded hip lines also showed off behind the *kain* that wrapped tightly around me from the calf to my waist. With a deep cleavage and bouncing hips, I must have looked very seductive when walking.

As more customers bought my jamu, Yu Ning and Yu Sih were no longer rivals. I was no longer concerned with my rough and unattractive face when men whistled at me as I walked past them. Instead, I confidently smiled while offering my jamu.

The men gathered around me like bees swarming around a flower. They raced to sit beside or in front of me, and tried to get as near as possible. When they drank my jamu they tried to touch my arm, peek into my cleavage, and pat my thighs. After a while I understood these were signs they wanted me.

Giggling, Yu Ning and Yu Sih told each other stories about the customers they slept with. Sometimes I heard them exchange tips on how to play with the men on the sleeping mat. They also exchanged recipes for heightening a customer's satisfaction. This extra service added to their meager profits from selling jamu alone.

Mas Wandi was different. I don't know if it was because he was the first man who touched, felt, and squeezed my breasts, or because I had fallen for him. The sensation of his touch gushed deep into my body. It even made my bones quiver. At night, I became restless when thinking about his strong muscles and body odor.

"What is it about me that excites you?" I asked coyly, wanting to give my all to him.

"Everything, little girl."

"Really?" I continued to flirt.

"Let me take you home tonight, okay?" He seemed to really want me.

I went home riding Mas Wandi's pedicab. He pedaled along the already quiet and dark Kembang Jepun, and passed the mansions owned by rich Chinese people along Kapasan Street. Near the railroad tracks on Kenjeran Street, he stopped. The place was deserted, with many trees and bushes. There were no streetlights.

Mas Wandi parked his pedicab at the curb, climbed into it, and sat beside me. His body was very close to mine. I felt his shoulder rub against mine when he put his arm around me. I was quiet in complete surrender, and waited for whatever pleasure he would give me.

In the darkness his steamy breath rushed down my neck and inside my ears. His hand slipped into my kebaya and fondled my breasts with a new hunger. This was not like the touches he did before. My breasts felt on fire in the grip of his palm.

Snorting and panting, he devoured my breasts. I wriggled with pleasure and enjoyed the sensation that made my female organ wet. He ripped off my kain and guided me to sit on his lap. Something hard penetrated my body. While it hurt, there was also pleasure. This did not last long. Something squirted inside me and mixed with my own reddened liquid.

The man gasped and slumped back. My body fell in his arms.

Mas Wandi had taken my virginity.

After that, he always took me home with his pedicab. He also gave me lessons in lovemaking. Mas Wandi was a mature man who knew a woman's nuts and bolts. He guided me patiently so we could achieve mutual satisfaction. We did it anywhere and anytime we saw an opportunity to have the pleasure. I was thirsty for his touch. He made me an adult woman.

Several months later I met Mas Sujono.

He was a coolie at the textile shop of Babah Oen, the richest Chinese on Coklat Street. Babah Oen was not only famous for owning three big textile shops and holding almost half of the textile trades on Gula Street, Coklat Street, and Kembang Jepun, he also had two big houses on Kapasan Street. Only the rich Chinese who could afford a guard lived there. Babah Oen was also known for being stingy and demanding.

I often went to the area of Chinese shops people called *Pecinan*, Chinatown, to sell my jamu. Coklat, Karet, Slompretan, and Kembang Jepun were known as the golden square. Mostly Chinese merchants controlled the area, especially Coklat Street, where most of the *batik* stores were located. Chinatown was a very busy, well-developed trade center supported by water transportation on Kali Mas River, where many commercial ships passed through. I had more customers in the area, not only ship coolies but also those who worked for the shops along the streets.

Babah Oen's coolies often bought my jamu, and Mas Sujono did, too. He always asked for the jamu that helps stiff muscles and increases a man's sex power with honey and an egg. Most often he did not pay. His excuse was that he had used all his money to buy cigarettes.

"Can I owe you? I'll pay next month," he said, giggling.

I don't know why I said yes to him; every time his debt was due he said, "next month." That month was followed with another "next month."

Was it because he stared at me so intensely that I felt he was stripping me naked? I was nervous when I caught him staring at my cleavage as I bent down, and blushed as he watched me when I was still at a distance. I knew he often looked at my legs as my kain split while walking. His sneaky, wild eyes made my heart pound faster.

Mas Sujono was different from Mas Wandi, who told me openly about his passion and desire. Mas Sujono expressed his passion through stolen glances, and his eyes had a hungry look when I caught him. No words of praise came from his thin-lipped mouth, but his fierce eyes made me unable to say no when he offered to accompany me home. I only knew him for a few months and things went quickly after I started paying attention to both men.

Two men, Mas Wandi and Mas Sujono.

Was it wrong? No, said my heart.

I did not want to be a pedicab driver's mistress. Although I was stupid and did not have a good education, I knew how much a pedicab driver like Mas Wandi earned and he still had to feed his wife and two children at home.

He slipped money in my bra because he wanted my body, but he could not afford to have me as a mistress. Mas Wandi did not earn enough from driving his pedicab to feed two families.

As long as he gave me money and I enjoyed making love with a mature person like him, what was wrong with meeting his needs? It gave me more pocket money and experience.

For my own life, I was like other girls who wanted to be a legal wife and not just a kept-woman. Mas Sujono had not yet married at the age of twenty-four. While he was thin, he had a muscular body. A coolie lifting rolls of textiles for a very rich Chinese had a fixed monthly salary, and this offered me the security I wanted. I could not rely on the unstable income of a pedicab driver. I did not see anything wrong with starting a romance with Mas Sujono.

One night he bit my lips while walking me home. I trembled because I felt the same passion. His kisses were steamy as he nibbled on my lips. He had a wild lust and I was naturally driven to kiss him back. We bit, nibbled, and sucked each other's lips and exchanged saliva. Sucking his lips gently, I realized how thin they were. I felt as if I had nothing to suck on.

After he released me, a stifling silence hung between us, interrupted by the faint sound of whizzing bullets.

"You're already good at kissing," he said.

Not knowing what he meant, I did not say anything.

Did he enjoy my response to him, or should I have pretended to be an innocent village girl who was receiving her first kiss?

"You and Mas Wandi often kiss each other, don't you?" he asked me frankly.

My customers whispered about my relationship with Mas Wandi, who took me home almost every evening. They said he showed affection to me, and had already told people I was his *istri muda*, or second wife.

"Oh yes, no," I sputtered. "There's nothing special between us."

He chuckled. "But that was not a usual kiss."

My cheeks burned. I could only repeat what I said.

What could I do? Mas Wandi slipped money into my bra, but Mas Sujono owed me for my jamu. Mas Wandi aroused my passion as a woman, while Mas Sujono gave me the wild lust of a man.

Two weeks afterward, I heard thumping on the door of the small room where I lived with Grandma. It was sometime after midnight. The size of the room was only four square-meters. We spread a mat on the floor to sleep on. Behind a bamboo partition in the back of the room was a small area where we put the stove and tools for cooking and making jamu. We washed ourselves and emptied our bowels in the bathrooms ten rooms away. There were only two bathrooms and two toilets for all the residents of the twelve rented rooms.

I lived in Surabaya with Grandma. Father and Mother were coolies who planted rice fields for Meneer Hansen, a Dutch landlord in Blitar, a village near Surabaya. The small wage they earned was just enough to eat for one day. I am the oldest child and I had five younger siblings. The youngest one still nursed. Our home in the village had a dirt floor, woven bamboo walls, and no rooms. The two bamboo beds had no mattresses. Father, Mother, and the youngest child shared one, while the other was for the rest of us. We slept like salted fish arranged side by side in a box.

Mother took me to Surabaya and entrusted me to Grandma when I was twelve years old. Before she left, she told me, "*Ndhuk*, go with Grandma to sell jamu."

I lived with Grandma since then. I cleaned our tiny room and did the washing while she sold jamu. She brought rice and tofu and tempeh, or sometimes fish and chili sauce, when she came home in the evening. We ate together. I had a great appetite as I had not eaten since morning and only filled my stomach with water. I had to be satisfied with white rice and sweet soy sauce when she could not sell her jamu.

"Who's there?" Grandma woke up, startled by the noise.

I opened the door to Mas Sujono, stinking of rice wine. He immediately pushed his way in. He panted and his eyes looked wild.

"A friend, Grandma," I replied.

"I'm drunk. Can't go home," Mas Sujono muttered.

Grandma looked at him perplexed. I had yet to introduce Mas Sujuno to her. I never thought he would come to my home in the middle of the night, and drunk. There was no way I could introduce him in such an indecent state.

He spoke in a nasal voice as if talking in his sleep. "Grandma, my apologies. I'm not feeling well. I can't go home. May I rest here?"

"Is your friend sick, Ndhuk? Please come in. I'll make you some jamu," Grandma said innocently and went to the back of the room.

I spread my sleeping mat on the floor and helped Mas Sujono lie down. He closed his eyes right away and I massaged his forehead. Drops of perspiration as large as rice grains showed on his forehead.

"Where have you been? Why did you get drunk?" I asked while I sat beside him and leaned against the wall.

"Bastards," he cursed.

"What happened?"

"Whore. Bitch. Bah," he continued.

"What happened, Mas?"

"I went to Kalimas. I just had rice wine, but the whore told people I slept with her and didn't want to pay. Bah. She screamed her head off calling me a thief. People chased me."

I did not know why I was jealous. I believed he belonged to me after we kissed that night, even though he had not said he loved me.

Not long after, Grandma came back with a glass of jamu and handed it to me. Seeing Mas Sujono was asleep, she said I should give it to him once he was awake and went back to her mat in the corner.

The room was murky in the lantern's light. Mas Sujono was on his back with his eyes shut, while Grandma snored softly. I held the glass of jamu, not knowing what to do since he did not stir.

Should I wake him, or should I wait? I wondered.

Would it be better if I went to sleep? Maybe so, but where should I lie down? I looked around the room. Grandma huddled like a kitten fast asleep in her corner, while Mas Sujono was on his back in mine. I decided to lie down next to Grandma and started to get up.

Mas Sujono moved. He grabbed my wrist, spilling the jamu, and jerked me down beside him. He opened his reddish eyes. "Where're you going?" he asked hoarsely.

"Go to sleep," I replied, a little scared.

"Sleep beside me."

I did not know what to say.

With one pull he made me fall and lie beside him. He lay on my body and pressed me down so I could not move. His panting breath blew on my face and his skin felt very hot on my skin. His breath smelled of rice wine.

He yanked at my chemise, popping the buttons and exposing my whole bosom. He bent his head and hungrily kissed my breasts. He was wild, fierce, and steamy. I wriggled. The overwhelming sensation made me unable to control my excitement. I trembled from the mixed feelings between fear and pleasure, confusion and desire, pain and lust.

I meant to say no, but the sound coming out of my mouth was a moan. My eyes were wide open and my body responded to his passion. I shifted my body when he parted my thighs with his feet and pressed me down harder. Like eels, his hands slithered over my entire body, and with a strong pull he ripped the kain from my hips. I was naked.

His hands squeezed my shoulders, breasts, hips, stomach, and further down. He treated me roughly, which made it more difficult to control myself. Confusion about whether I should stop or give in overwhelmed me. Mas Wandi never made love as wild as this. He always treated me gently and waited until we both achieved the peak of pleasure. What I felt now with Mas Sujono was different: wildness, hunger, and thirst. It was not warm, but burning hot.

While I battled my instincts and arousal, something slipped between my thighs. It painfully thrust inside me. My body quivered from unfinished desire as I felt my groin wet with warm liquid.

Mas Sujono relaxed and his breath slowed. He fell on his back with his eyes shut and snored.

Soon complete quiet spread and dead silence hung in the air. A falling needle would have sounded louder than a Nippon bomb. I drifted in and out of sleep until finally the morning came.

*****

I did not have my period the following month. I felt dizzy, weak, and kept vomiting. Although I was only sixteen, I knew something was wrong. I was scared and looked for Mas Sujono.

"Why are you looking for me?"

"I'm pregnant, Mas."

"What does it have to do with me?' he replied indifferently.

"You're the one who made me pregnant."

"How can you accuse me of that? You also slept with Mas Wandi," he shouted. "Why don't you go find him?"

The truth was that I did not know whose child I carried since both men had given me their seed. I did not know who had made me pregnant. If I chose to marry Mas Sujono, it was not because I knew the baby was his, but because I was embarrassed to have a husband as old as my father. I also did not want to be Mas Wandi's second wife and live poorly because I had to share his income with his family.

I was sick of living in poverty and always having to share. I already had enough poverty since I was born.

"I only did it with you," I said, and tried to make an excuse.

"You still sleep with Mas Wandi," he argued.

I chased Mas Sujono for days and he avoided me, while Mas Wandi chased me.

"Are you pregnant, Ndhuk?" he asked. "Sujono told me."

"No," I tried to hide my anger.

"Don't lie."

"No."

"Whose child is that, Ndhuk? You slept with Sujono besides doing it with me. You know the father."

"It's my own," I snapped.

"Don't lie," he repeated.

Hearing his gentle voice, I could not control my emotions. My eyes burned, my chest was stuffy, and my throat choked.

"What do you want, Mas?" I asked him in a brittle voice, trying not to cry.

"If that's really my child, I'll marry you, Ndhuk. I'll care for you." His voice was soft but firm.

I burst out crying.

Why did I meet a good man like Mas Wandi and be with him at the wrong time? Why did he have to be as old as my father? He already had a wife and two children. Why was he only a pedicab driver without a steady income? Why did he want to marry me? I did not have any feelings for him, and only needed his money and warmth. I never had any desire to be his wife.

I hoped to build my future with Mas Sujono. He was not rich like a priyayi, but decent enough for a husband. We were about the same age and he was not bad looking. He had a steady job, and was manly.

Mas Sujono did not want to accept any responsibility, but did he need to when I did not know whose baby was in my womb?

"No, it isn't yours, Mas Wandi," I said. I wanted to make Mas Sujono marry me.

Who would marry me if it became known I was no longer a virgin and pregnant? Pedicab drivers on West and East Kalimas Street knew of my relationship with Mas Wandi; clerks at the Chinese shops knew of my relationship with Mas Sujono.

No man would marry me. With an illegitimate child, I would be poorer because I'd have to feed the child alone, and be the topic of gossip for every woman in the tenement.

My fears haunted me while my stomach grew bigger, racing with the time. Mas Sujono avoided me and I could not confront his parents; his mother died when giving birth to him and his father had gone God knows where. People said he had remarried but did not want to see Mas Sujono because he considered him unlucky. Mas Sujono had lived with his maiden aunt since he was a child. I did not see any other way but to call on her. My fear gave me courage. With a stomach starting to bulge, I looked for her room in one of the shanties near Wonokromo train station, very far from my home in Kalimas. Wonokromo lies at the border of Surabaya on the banks of the Jagir River. We called the place "Jabakota," which means outside the city, because it was on the border of Surabaya. Fortunately, there was a tram that connected Kalimas with Wonokromo.

I reached her room at dusk, just before the *maghrib*, Muslim praying time. The sky was grey with red hues. Darkness started spreading its gloomy blanket and the crickets and frogs along Jagir River seemed to be competing to make loud noises. The flickering lights of kerosene lamps fluttered like fireflies through the holes in the walls.

"Who are you, Ndhuk? What can I do for you? Sujono hasn't returned yet," his aunt said when receiving me.

"I'm Sulis, Auntie. I'm looking for Mas Sujono because it's difficult to see him where he works. I'm pregnant with his child."

The news confused the middle-aged woman for several minutes. Her mouth opened and closed as if she wanted to say something but nothing came out. She looked at me closely. I did not know if it was to examine me or because the lantern light was not bright enough for her to see me.

"Sujono never told me about you, Ndhuk. He is going to marry Sutini, *Kang* Paimin's daughter. He is our neighbor. We'll have the wedding in the month of *Besar* next year," she said.

I was shocked. I could not let it happen. My heart screamed.

"Excuse me, Auntie, but Sutini's not pregnant, is she? I'm expecting your nephew's child."

"But."

"There is no 'but,' Auntie. I am willing to apologize to Sutini if necessary."

"I don't know, Ndhuk. You'd better wait for Sujono."

"I'm sorry, Auntie. I won't go home until he marries me." I heard the sadness in my voice, but I was determined.

Not long afterward, Mas Sujono arrived. He was startled when he saw me in his tiny home. His facial expressions kept changing.

Auntie broke the silence. "Sujono, Sulis has been waiting for you since maghrib."

"What are you doing here?" he snapped angrily.

"You've to marry me, Mas. I'm pregnant with your child."

"No."

I no longer held my tears and they soon flowed down my face.

Why was the man so wicked? My heart hurt. He had tasted all of my body, and I enjoyed what we did because we both wanted it. Making love with him was more exciting than with Mas Wandi, who had started to lose his vigor. Mas Sujono never paid a cent for my jamu or for sleeping with me. He took advantage of me to get pleasure. Now he wanted to wash his hands of any responsibility. Oh, don't think you can get rid of me that easy.

"I won't go home. I'll stay here until you marry me," I said loudly.

"What do you want?" he shouted, looking outside the room.

It was very quiet as if the town was dead. Through the room's thin wall a sigh or a woman's scream could be easily heard.

"It's your child, Mas. You've got to be responsible. I'll tell everyone in the *kampung* if necessary." I started to raise my voice. My mind was numb. I had to have him.

"You're mad," he snarled.

We started arguing and soon we were fighting. He raised his voice while I began shouting. He evaded; I demanded.

One by one people came to watch, until they numbered ten, twenty, thirty, men and women, old and young. They crowded the front door and whispered to each other. This was free entertainment, and more fun than hiding in a room and being scared at the sounds of whizzing bullets, marching soldiers, roaring airplanes, and rattling war vehicles.

"Go home, go. You're making me ashamed."

"No. I'll stay until you marry me."

He pulled me roughly out of the room.

"Help," I yelled, determined to stay.

"Oh my God," his auntie screamed in panic.

Mas Sujono still tried dragging me, but I refused to move.

"You're an untrustworthy man," I bawled.

The people watching became noisy and moved closer. Some restrained Mas Sujono and others held me. In the uproar, people asked questions, made comments, grumbled, and even swore at me. They sounded like buzzing bees.

Finally, a middle-aged man pushed through the crowd. He was actually not very old but looked authoritative because of his grey hair.

"What's going on? All of you should be inside. The situation is critical and unpredictable. What if there was a gunfight when you're all here making a commotion?" he shouted.

Everyone quieted.

"What's going on, Auntie?"

"This girl is Sulis. She said she lives in Kalimas. She has waited for Sujono since maghrib. She said she's pregnant with Sujono's child." Her voice trembled.

The middle-aged man looked at me.

I wiped my tears with the back of my hand when our eyes met. I felt scared, worried, tired and bitter. Tears streamed down my face.

"Is it true that Sujono has made you pregnant, Ndhuk?"

I nodded.

I heard a slap and then there was a deep silence. The man had hit Mas Sujono, who covered his cheek with his palm but could not conceal all of the red mark.

"Bastard," the man shouted.

"But *Pak…*"

"Fortunately you haven't married Sutini. Fortunately we've discovered this disgrace. How my daughter would have suffered if we found out after you married her."

It turned out that he was Sutini's father.

I could not help smirking and cheering triumphantly inside my heart. What parent would give his daughter to a man who has made another woman pregnant? I felt victory would be mine.

"You have to marry this girl."

"But Pak, I'm not sure the child is mine. Sulis is also seeing another man."

I heard another loud noise. Sutini's father had punched Sujono.

"Be a man, not a coward. She wouldn't have chased you here if she were not sure you're the father."

"Pak, please, let me speak."

"Don't make excuses," the man interrupted.

I felt as if a fresh breeze was coming toward me. I had support.

"Pak, I love Sutini."

"I won't let you marry her."

I had almost won.

"Marry this girl now. Don't be a disgrace."

I really won, my heart shouted.

We were married that night without a traditional ceremony, party, festivity, dowry, or wedding complexities like those in a priyayi wedding. There was only resentment, which, I believed, piled up in Mas Sujono's mind.

He did not look at me. His thin lips formed a straight line and anger burned like fire in his eyes but I did not care. At least I had saved myself.

*****

After we got married, Mas Sujono moved into my tiny room with Grandma. The room seemed smaller with three people. As my stomach grew bigger, I still sold jamu and went from one street to another along the sidewalk. The scorching sun made my body wet with sweat.

Meanwhile, Mas Sujono worked for Babah Oen carrying textile rolls for a monthly wage. The money never reached me because he spent it on cigarettes, getting drunk on rice wine at the end of the alley, and gambling. After working for about two or three months, he wanted to quit.

"I'm tired of being a coolie. I want to be a soldier defending the country," he said when I asked why he did not go to work.

The country was in a mess with the war going on and the Nippon invading our islands. I had heard the Nippon wanted to help Indonesian soldiers get independence from the Dutch. They said they were the elder brothers of the Indonesian people.

Maybe what the Nippon said was true. Their eyes and hair are black, just like Indonesians and not the Dutch, who have blue eyes and hair like corn silk. I also heard the Nippon ate rice instead of bread and potatoes like the Dutch. They were not as tall as the Dutch, and looked more like us except with narrower eyes.

Shootings and bomb explosions happened everywhere, and every day. We were always ready for evacuation when the siren wailed. Surabaya turned into a dead city. No one went out of the house. Newspapers and the radio said the Dutch were cornered but they did not want to give up Indonesia to the Nippon, so we lived with the sounds of whizzing bullets. It was not clear who fought, the Dutch against the Nippon or the Dutch against Indonesians. It was also not clear whether the Nippon were fighting with the Indonesian soldiers or they fought on their own.

None of this was important to me, but very important to Mas Sujono.

He liked to sit all day listening to news about the war from a neighbor's radio while smoking his cigarettes. He made comments on the Dutch troops, who were losing. It seemed the Nippon would soon take over Surabaya. He was very enthusiastic about the Indonesian youths who joined the armed struggle.

"The people fighting for independence are heroes," he said.

"Will we no longer be poor when this country is free?" I asked cynically. "Can the people you call heroes give us food? We will still have to work to feed ourselves, won't we? That's why you need to go to Babah Oen soon and ask him for work. You haven't worked for a month," I grumbled.

"What's most important is this country's freedom. Indonesia is much bigger than a jamu peddler's basket," he replied nonchalantly.

"I'm giving birth soon. We'll need money."

"We?" he asked, lifting his eyebrows.

"Yes, we, for giving birth."

"So?"

"You have to work to get money for the expenses." I started raising my voice.

"How come? I married you because you trapped me. The child may not be mine. Why is it me who has to work?"

I screamed, unable to hold my tears. The answers from the man I had hoped to trust with my life were only trash.

I thought he was a man who would meet the needs of a wife and children, a man willing to work hard for the family. I did not dream of a luxurious life like a priyayi who wore nice-smelling kebayas. I did not want be a vice regent's wife who always wore new kains, or a Dutch wife who ate expensive meals everyday.

I just wanted Mas Sujono to have a steady job. Any kind of work would do as long as I did not have to worry about our rice pot everyday. Moreover, I would soon have our baby—or my baby.

I honestly did not know which man was the father of the child in my womb, Mas Sujono or Mas Wandi. I knew Mas Wandi before Mas Sujono, and Mas Wandi had taken my virginity. Both men had slept with me and I enjoyed it because they offered different things I wanted.

I never thought it would end like this. Marriage with Mas Sujono felt like a thorn in the flesh. He was a lazy drunk who did not want to care for us because he was not sure if the child was his.

After maghrib, he would waste time at the corner of the alley, gambling and drinking rice wine until he was drunk. Once drunk, he looked for trouble and quarreled with other people before coming home dirty and smelly. He banged on the door as if he wanted to wake up everyone in the kampung. After retching very loudly and vomiting the contents of his stomach, he slept until noon.

Rather than think about his duties as a husband and father-to-be, Mas Sujono was preoccupied with his unrealized dream of being a soldier. I did not want him to be a soldier, especially in this unstable country. I'd rather he worked at any other job.

"If not for you, I'd carry a rifle, be fighting for the country, defending it, and struggling for independence. I'd be a respected person instead of a coolie who lifts textile rolls at a Chinese shop. I don't have tall dreams to become a general or president. I just want to help the country get its independence. Is that wrong?" he said wryly when I pointed out his weaknesses.

For me, it was more important to think about our stomachs than independence. Many smart people took care of this country's business, and enough soldiers were already fighting. Being concerned for your wife and child was more important, wasn't it?

When I was six months pregnant, the gossip among our neighbors about Mas Sujono heightened. They said he was jobless and could only squat in Grandma's room. It upset him when he heard it, but instead of feeling embarrassed and guilty, he challenged them to fight. Although my stomach was already big, I asked him to move us to another rented room in the next alley.

My pregnancy advanced, my legs became heavier, and I could no longer carry the basket on my back to sell jamu. My feet were also swollen, but I did not see any change in Mas Sujono. He did not care about my condition or that we fasted when we had nothing to eat.

I finally gave birth to a boy. With much fear I pushed him out of my womb into our poverty.

I was very anxious when the boy was born. What if he was the son of Mas Wandi? What would I say to Mas Sujono? Would he divorce me? I would be a young divorcee who had to support a child during a very unpredictable time. Why did poverty love me so much? Why did it never go away from me?

Oh God… I wept without tears.

The Lord still had mercy and took pity on my suffering. My baby did not resemble either man. I had passed all I had to the boy, a square jaw, big eyes, and a wide mouth. I no longer cared whether he was the child of Mas Sujono or Mas Wandi.

Mas Sujono did not turn toward the boy, let alone help name him. I am not someone with a good education or of royal blood, so I did not know what to call my son. I finally named him Joko. It meant he was a boy, a very simple name.

I hoped Mas Sujono would be more responsible now that we had a child. With Joko's arrival, I could no longer sell jamu because I had to take care of him. Mas Sujono had to work harder since we had another mouth to feed.

The days, months, and finally the year passed by without any change. We remained very poor. At night I wondered what we'd eat the following day, and when the morning came I worried if there would be anything to eat at night. Everyday was the same.

I was sick of poverty. I hated suffering.

Poverty had been in front of my eyes since I breathed for the first time. My father was dark and skinny, and my mother's breasts sagged from nursing six children without much time between the births. When they considered me old enough to look after my younger siblings, Mother worked as a rice field coolie to feed us. I used to share rice with my younger siblings, and we were lucky to have rice without any side dish. It was better than filling our stomachs with water all day. I also wore the same clothes for days until they turned filthy. Then I washed them at night and as soon as the morning sun had dried them, I wore them again.

Being sent to Surabaya to live with Grandma was a relief. I was determined to stay away from poverty. I did not want to marry a farmer who worked on someone else's rice field. I wanted nice clothes and not have to share one piece of tempeh with my siblings rather than fight over it.

Seeing my husband's behavior made me angrier. We fought almost every day. Sometimes our fights were as fierce as the Indonesian militia's uprising against the Dutch.

According to an announcement from my neighbor's radio, the country was hit by an economic crisis. The Dutch loss against the Nippon brought many changes. The Nippon now controlled Surabaya and the surrounding area. On the morning of March 8, 1942 the commander-in-chief of the Royal Netherlands East Indies Army surrendered to the Nippon. That same afternoon, the Dutch governor, along with other officials, met with the Nippon commander-in-chief at Kalijati, West Java, and agreed to the surrender of all Dutch troops. Although the Dutch soldiers bragged they would rather die than yield to Japan's Imperial government, they lay down their arms after only seven days of fighting.

Indonesians had put their hopes on the Nippon, who proclaimed themselves as our elder brothers. As the younger brothers, we hoped to have a better life. We praised the Nippon and happily welcomed them into our country.

This did not last long. I saw the number of poor people increase. Open, hungry mouths were everywhere. We only had sweet potatoes and cassava to eat because the harvested rice had to be sold to the Nippon rice-buying organization. Even farmers did not have rice to eat or seeds to plant. The organization also bought chicken eggs very cheaply; they said these were for the Indonesian soldiers who had joined the Nippon-sponsored volunteer militia known as PETA. Meanwhile, the marching boots, whizzing bullets, and rattling tanks of the Nippon were indifferent to the starving people.

We were forced to pay our respects to their flag. Our red and white flag was replaced with a flag with a red circle in the center, which they called *Hinomaru*, and we were forced to sing *Kimigayo*, the Japanese national anthem, and do the *seikeirei*—a ninety-degree bow to respect the Japanese emperor.

What was worse, many Indonesians had to work as *romusha*, forced laborers, which made them suffer beyond words. The Nippon praised them as labor heroes, but actually hundred thousands of Indonesian people were taken away and forced to work. They built war bunkers at beaches and on mountains. Many of them were also taken to Burma and Thailand to build railroads.

Under the burning sun they carried sand and stones without enough food and rest. They looked like walking skeletons. Their very weak bodies would stagger and fall, and instead of getting help, they were shouted at and hit. They had to scramble to get drinking water from a good well; if there was none, they drank water from the river they used for bathing and defecating as there were no toilets. They slept outside since the Nippon did not provide tents, and were always wet and cold from rains and the humid night air. Worse, swarms of mosquitoes attacked them. Soon, bones wrapped in skin were everywhere, shaking, talking deliriously, and screaming in pain from malaria and dysentery. Instead of being given medicine, they were forced to keep working. Within a short time, the laborers turned into abandoned corpses.

People became very frightened when they saw Nippon soldiers. They were scared their rice harvest and eggs would be confiscated. They were also afraid their husbands and sons would be forced into being romushas. Young women hid for fear that they would be taken away to be *jugun ianfus*—comfort women for the Nippon soldiers. I no longer saw cheerful faces like when the Nippon defeated the Dutch. People's eyes looked empty. There was no light in them, and this did not only happen to Indonesians.

The Chinese also hated the Nippon. In retaliation for their invasion of China and the suffering they had afflicted on the Chinese people, the Chinese boycotted the Nippon. Many closed their shops and would not do any business with them. Chinese schools stopped their activities.

Maybe the hurt Chinese people had in their hearts were like the stabbing wounds the Dutch made in the chests of Indonesian people. Occupation, wherever it is, always causes pain, doesn't it?

But Sulis remained Sulis the uneducated. Living in the clutch of poverty, I remained Sulis who did not have any spirit of nationalism. I was more concerned with how to feed my son than economic recession. I did not understand what the words meant. I only knew my son needed rice everyday. I did not care if the flag that waved on the pole was Dutch or Nippon; my life and that of my son were more important.

But Mas Sujono did not want to know about it.

"I'm not working. Where would I get money from?" he responded when I complained about having no money for our daily needs.

"Find a job, a steady one, Mas."

"What job, as a romusha? Fuck! You want me to die soon, don't you?" he shouted. "The Nippon promise to help Indonesia get independence was a lie. We have to rebel against them and demand the independence they promised."

"Mas, that's the business of the clever people who are leading the revolution and thinking about independence. What we need to think about is that we have to keep eating. Find work, any kind of work. We don't have any money to buy food. We can fast, but Joko has to eat."

"Ask your lover, Wandi, for money. It's his child. Why do you ask me to work to feed him?" He puffed his hand-rolled cigarette, not even looking at me.

"Joko is your child."

Mas Sujono did not care what I said. "If you need money, go back to work and sell jamu. Don't ask me for it."

I swallowed the bitterness, all of it. I was insulted but what could I do?

With the skills of making jamu I had learned from Grandma, I took my bottles, basket, and the cloth to fasten it on my back. I sold jamu while leaving Joko with Grandma until the evening.

Every day I returned to our rented room in the tenement near the time of maghrib, I would be exhausted. My back was sore from carrying the various bottles of jamu in my basket, my feet blistered from walking very far, and my skin was sticky with sweat.

Piles of chores waited for me: dirty clothes, cooking, cleaning, and boiling betel leaves, turmeric, king of bitters, palm sugar, and salt to prepare the jamu for the next day, as well as serving Mas Sujono on the sleeping mat.

He never wanted to know how tired I was. He was only interested in whether I had made everything he wanted, from a glass of coffee in the morning to meals, and accepted his rough lovemaking.

Making love? I could not call it that anymore.

Was it making love if I had to serve him when my whole body felt tired? Were we intimate if our union did not end with both of us satisfied? Was it a huddle for warmth if I was already half asleep and just let him "work" by himself?

When he finished, when everything was finished, we would start another round of fighting over anything he thought about.

"Why do you sleep all the time?" he grumbled when I did not respond to his groping.

"Tired."

"From sleeping with those short, slanted-eyed Nippon?" he sneered.

People knew how rough Nippon soldiers were to Indonesian women. They abused many of us. To them, women were objects that serviced their lust—even if it meant rape. Parents no longer let their daughters out of the house in fear the soldiers would take them away and make them sex slaves.

"How can you say such a thing? I'm tired from selling jamu, Mas," I sulked.

"So you are more concerned with selling jamu than serving me?" he started his senseless argument.

"You asked me to go back to work." I was sick of arguing. It seemed as if it wasn't enough I worked all day long, I could not even have a good night's sleep.

Mas Sujono was clever in finding things to fight over. Sometimes he made things up to start a row, especially when he came home drunk. Even the most trivial things could make us start arguing. He preferred fighting to thinking about what we would eat the next day.

Mas Sujono got up. Bare-chested, he walked to the back. Soon I heard the sound of breaking bottles. I gritted my teeth to hold my anger. I got up and followed him. My jamu bottles, which kept us eating, were shattered.

"How will I work tomorrow? If we had enough money to eat, I wouldn't have to peddle jamu." I glared at him.

The longer I lived with him the more defiant I became. Mas Sujono said I was more and more disrespectful. He hated me glaring at him. He said it was not appropriate for a wife to behave like that to her husband.

He deserved it. He showed no responsibility as the head of the family and I respected him less and less as the days went by.

His fist shot out and punched me in my eye. "Don't stare at me."

I staggered, swayed, and covered my face crying out in pain, but the hurt in my heart was a wound I could not nurse by weeping. I fell on the floor.

While still in pain and not fully conscious, Mas Sujono leapt on me like a hungry tiger. He pulled my legs up in the air, pressed them against my chest, and pushed me until my head hit the wall. I whimpered and tears flooded my face, but he did not care. He penetrated me roughly until his sweat fell like a mist. He stopped without the squirt of the warm liquid.

He had raped me.

The pain made me feel as if all my joints were loose and my bones broken. But strangely, while he manhandled me I felt a new sensation. I was satisfied. I enjoyed it.

Since we married, I had turned into the slave he needed to wash his clothes, cook, and make him coffee. I always had to fight about our lack of money. Our times on the mat had turned dull when I realized there would never be love between us, never a return to the passionate lovemaking from our early days together. Mas Sujono never made love tenderly like Mas Wandi. Mas Sujono wanted to release his lust his own way. He did not care if I was having my period.

I felt lower than a whore.

I had a child but never felt like a true wife to Mas Sujono. He was very selfish. He never cared if his wife and child could eat as long as he had cigarettes to smoke. His thin-lipped mouth was always talking, cursing, and abusing. He treated me no different from a handmaid who made him coffee. He was also very violent. Besides rice, I had his punches on my plate. He was rough not only with his words and hands, but also when sleeping with me.

What I had just felt, which made me satisfied, was not love or affection. It was simply wild, raw lust. The man had penetrated me with his eyes burning red, puffing like a train and pouring sweat, and only stopped when he had exhausted his rage, without satisfaction.

Was he like an animal? I don't know. The sex instinct of humans is most like an animal's, isn't it?

"That was to teach you not to gawk at me." He turned his back and went to sleep as if nothing had happened.

Ours was a wrong marriage, one that imprisoned me in the clutches of the wrong man. Mas Sujono was obsessed with his fantasies, thoughtless and violent, and had a bad mouth.

If I had to continue serving a man like that on our sleeping mat, would there be room left in my heart for any form of love?

I did not know what love was like anymore, if it was shaped like a heart, square, triangle, or had no shape at all.

Young Dutch women and men said the color of love was pink. That's only what people in love would say. To me, love was pitch black, or maybe white, not because it was sacred but because it was blank.

People said love is beautiful because it is sweet and pliable because it has a shape. It did not make any difference to me if love actually tasted sweet or bitter, was beautiful or ugly, or pliable or hard. To me, love was just trouble.

The next day I had black eyes and felt like all my bones were broken. I could not get up from the mat. My eyes were swollen because of Mas Sujono's punches and crying all night.

"I'm going to see Babah Oen for work," he said, and left the room without looking at me.

Mas Sujono went back to lifting textile rolls at the shop. As a temporary worker, he was only paid every two weeks, but it kept us from starving.

I did not sell jamu again. I should have been happy, but it made me feel imprisoned. My days were longer as time passed very slowly. I took care of Joko and served Mas Sujono with an increasingly boring routine of making him coffee in the morning, cooking, washing his clothes, and sleeping with him.

All I saw were the four walls of our tiny room, and all I heard were my son's whimpers. There was nothing to do except the boring house chores, which I no longer saw as duties. I was a puppet driven by the fear of getting hit and punched. The only thing I sometimes enjoyed was having sex, during which he performed wildly.

Things turned strange during the last three months. First, we were never short of money anymore. I did not have to have a headache from scrounging money for the day's food. We always had enough rice and Mas Sujono had his cigarettes. While we were still poor, our stove was always warm. We no longer had to eat our rice with only sweet soy sauce. We never had meat, but we enjoyed tofu, tempeh, eggs, crackers, and dried salted fish, which were luxuries to us.

I never knew where Mas Sujono got the money. He worked when he liked at Babah Oen's shop, and the time he started was not predictable. He came home late at night, more often just before sunrise.

I knew something was wrong, but I didn't worry about it. My marriage was not right from the beginning anyway. Another problem would not be unusual. Moreover, the new problem had solved our previous ones. I did not need to worry about it.

Where the money came from didn't matter because I had never felt like a true wife to Mas Sujono. He treated me like a slave who had to serve him, including in bed. As a slave, or even as a prostitute, I deserved payment.

His needs in bed were another thing that disturbed me.

Mas Sujono came home drunk almost every night, but the smell of alcohol was not like the usual one. Mixed with the odor of sweat on his clothes was a hint of fragrance.

During those months he only slept with me twice. This had never happened before. He would have sex with me at least once every two days.

Now we had only done it twice in three months. When we did, he was drunk and called out, "Matsumi."

Matsumi was not an Indonesian name, or Javanese. Who was she? The question bothered me.

So I asked Mas Sujono. "Mas, you called for Matsumi in your sleep. Who is she?" or, "Mas, where have you been? Why didn't you come home last night?" or, "Mas, where are you working? Are you still at Babah Oen's shop?"

Every time I asked about Matsumi or the money, we fought. It always ended with my face getting bruised from his punch.

"Stop talking so much. You kept harassing me for money, didn't you? Now I've given you enough, so shut up," he said, dismayed, as if I did not have the right to ask.

I became used to not caring about our problems as long as we had food to fill our stomachs. Eating is more important than love, which I never knew to be anything other than a release of lust.

There was no love between Mas Sujono and me, only lust when we wrestled on the mat. It was not a man and a woman uniting, but two animals fighting.

All we had were difficulties. Mas Sujono was a difficult man, and I was trapped in a difficult marriage. I felt bored, fed up, and sick and tired of the poverty that strangled me like the grip of a giant snake, slowly breaking every bone in my body.

Now the difficulties were gone, and I could enjoy life. Why didn't I just enjoy it? Was I wicked, cunning, or evil like *Durna*?

No, I was only Sulis, until the giant snake got me into trouble.

Part 2: Tjoa Kim Hwa

Surabaya, 1942

The Golden Flower Snake

Pale clouds in a bleak sky greeted me in Surabaya, and the breeze felt dry on my face as the ship docked at Tanjung Perak Harbor. At least I no longer swayed like I did at sea. I wanted a bath. Sticky salt dust covered my body and I had to see Shosho, Major General Kobayashi.

I came from Jakarta, where I had stayed with Itsuka-san, the owner of the Okamura shop at the corner of Kwitang Street. People in Jakarta called him "Tuan Toko," or Mr. Shop. He sold a variety of Japanese goods in his small store, anything from stationary to clothing to toys. It was busy everyday with local people who liked inexpensive but quality Japanese merchandise. They shopped there because they could not afford the more expensive Dutch stores.

Tuan Toko was also well liked. He was very friendly and polite to his customers, and always thanked them with a big smile and a deep bow.

"We are brothers," he said to his customers. "Japan is Indonesia's older brother."

Was this true? I did not know. I only knew Shosho Kobayashi had been in the country for some time—he said it was for a trade negotiation. He asked me to wait in Jakarta until he called me to Surabaya.

I looked among the people who swarmed the port but did not see him. Instead there were many bare-chested coolies carrying cargo from the docked ships.

Groups of Chinese scrambled to get off ships, one from Jakarta, and another commercial ship with a Chinese flag. Their faces looked as shabby as their clothes, with heavy narrow eyes and dirty skin. They crowded the decks like salted fish being dried in the sun. Many had gone without eating for days as they did not have food on board and they could not afford to buy anything to fill their stomachs at the ports of call. Still they were determined to get to Java.

Itsuka-san said that the Chinese came to Java because Japan invaded their homeland and had occupied Manchuria since 1931. Our soldiers paralyzed the Chinese troops, bombarded their villages, and burned people's rice fields, farmlands, and houses. Smoke filled the air and dead bodies were scattered everywhere. Chinese soldiers were arrested and shot, while girls and women were taken away. Most were taken to Japan and the countries under its occupation. They were turned into comfort women to fulfill the Japanese soldiers' need for female companionship during the fierce war.

The Japanese government gave the Manchu emperor's throne to Pu Yi, the last Chinese emperor, who fled when the country became a republic in 1912.

After Japan took over Manchuria, its government changed to the system ordered by the occupying army. Japanese stores and restaurants opened with white doorway curtains and *kanji* writings. Japanese women wearing wooden clogs tapped along the streets, paying no attention to the Chinese women in rags.

Itsuka-san tried to fill my ears with his politics. Western civilization penetrated China and a confrontation developed between the Kuomintang Party and the Chinese Communist Party. Zhang Xueliang released Chiang Kai-shek, the head of Kuomintang government, on the condition he unite with the Communist Party to take Manchuria back from the Japanese. But Chiang Kai-shek chose to establish Taiwan as a nation rather than join China under the Communist flag, and poverty became more widespread in China.

I did not understand all the political stories Itsuka-san told me. I only knew the Chinese were very poor and trying to better their lives overseas, including the island of Java.

Chinese people started to settle on Java a long time ago and had spread to all corners of Central Java, East Java, and even to the island of Madura. Some of them married indigenous people, including Javanese royalty. Numerous Chinese immigrants married local women and converted into Islam, the religion of many Javanese. The Dutch colonial government appointed several of them as *kapitan*, the head of the Chinese community in Surabaya, Malang, Pasuruan, Gresik, and Probolinggo. During the 1800s, a member of the Han family bought a piece of land in Panarukan and Besuki from Governor General Daendels for about 400,000 *spaansche matten*. Not long after, a kapitan from Pasuruan also bought land in Probolinggo from Daendels and received the title *Majoor der Chineezen en Landheer van Probolinggo,* or Major of the Chinese and Land Baron of Probolinggo. He was later appointed as the regent of the area but better known as "Babah Tumenggung." Because of this history, it seemed normal the people in China felt a connection to the immigrants and were attracted to Java. Large groups headed for the island, where they traded and assimilated with the native population. The Japanese occupation of China caused widespread poverty and the influx of immigrants to Java was undeniable. Every ship that dropped anchor at a Javanese port was filled with Chinese passengers. Their arrival was like the surge of a tidal wave during a storm.

I still looked for Shosho Kobayashi in the milling crowd, but all I saw were Chinese people on the move. Some were met by family but most took care of themselves. Coolies carried merchandise and war equipment from the ships. With chaos and harried people wherever I looked, I started to worry.

A young man approached me. Unlike the shabbily dressed Chinese, he wore neat clothes. He was not Javanese since he had olive skin and slanted eyes. He bowed deeply.

"Tjoa Kim Hwa-san?" he asked with a Japanese accent.

My heart jumped.

"Where is Shosho Kobayashi?"

"He's busy. I was asked to meet you," he whispered, anxiously looking around. "The situation is volatile. You'd better not mention Kobayashi-san's name. Follow me."

I looked at him. It was very strange he did not mention Shosho Kobayashi's title. He also knew me by the name Itsuka-san gave me when I left Jakarta.

Itsuka-san told me in Jakarta, "Last night Shosho Kobayashi sent a message through a courier. A commercial ship will sail for Surabaya in two days, and a berth is reserved in your new name. According to Shosho Kobayashi, everything is almost done."

What was done? I wondered. It must be the trade negotiations.

I recalled my conversation with Itsuka-san.

"Oh yes, once you arrive in Surabaya, your name is Tjoa Kim Hwa. Remember, Tjoa Kim Hwa," he said in a stern tone while I remained confused.

"Whose name is that?"

"Yours. I found a name as beautiful as your face. Kim Hwa means golden flower."

"What about Tjoa?"

"Tjoa could mean snake."

"Golden Flower Snake?" The name was scary.

The flower represents beauty and is a fitting symbol for women, while gold represents something precious and valuable. It was indeed an amazing name. But why a snake, a venomous animal that strikes and kills?

"Tjoa is also a Chinese surname," Itsuka-san explained as if he could read my mind. He apparently knew I did not like the name from my tone of voice.

"Why should I use Tjoa? I have my own surname."

"In Surabaya you must pass as Chinese. Don't let people know you're Japanese. You are the geisha Shosho Kobayashi favored in Japan and he wants you with him in Surabaya. You have to disguise yourself."

I could not imagine being a Chinese woman. They rarely bathed and always looked dirty; they stank and had bad breath. I had seen bits of food stuck between their teeth. Their feet were bound in accordance to a government policy that decreed women's feet be small, so small they could not walk sprightly, let alone run. They liked to shout in loud and rough voices, too.

Chinese women dared to stare into a man's eyes. They wore simple clothes with dull colors and only wore a new dress—bright red—on New Year's Day.

Japanese women really love to bathe. It is a must for us. We clean our bodies with soap, flush the dirt away with water, and then soak in the *ofuro*. Our feet are not bound; we walk gracefully by taking quick small steps on our clogs, which make a pleasant sound when we walk across a graveled path. We also revere our men and never look them in the eye. We bow to them and keep our eyes on the dust at the tips of their shoes. When we do look at a man, we do this from behind the wide sleeves of our *kimonos*. The kimono with its *obi* also has brilliant colors.

How could I pretend to be a Chinese woman?

"Geishas only exist in Japan. If a Japanese woman is a hostess overseas, it lowers our dignity as a country. Remember, we are one of the most important countries in the world. Our country will lead Asia."

I did not need to argue. The most important thing was meeting Shosho Kobayashi.

Itsuka-san whispered to the captain as I boarded the ship to Surabaya. I could not hear what he said but the captain nodded. Special treatment was mine during the voyage, with enough to eat and drink, and not being squeezed between Chinese people with their bad body odor and bad breath. Now that I had arrived, Shosho Kobayashi still could not see me. Instead he sent the young man. Whether I liked it or not, I had no other choice but to follow him.

I had no idea where he would take me. We got into a car and once we were out of the harbor, I saw a deserted road of worn asphalt. Our car was the only motorized vehicle. The rest were only bicycles, ox and horse-drawn carts, and three-wheeled carriages the man called *becak*.

We arrived at a large house with many rooms. The great room was huge, with chairs and short-legged tables arranged like in a Japanese restaurant. Several young women walked between the tables, their faces white with powder and bright red lips. They wore *yukata,* summer kimonos. Some had fair skin and slanted eyes, but many were dark and big-eyed.

"This is the dormitory of an entertainment club—a *kurabu*. We're accommodating the girls until they become hostesses. They come from China, Java, and Korea," the man said to answer my curiosity.

"You'll stay here for a while. You can do everything you like, except receive a male guest until Kobayashi-san comes to see you. He has arranged everything."

"Are they *maiko*, geisha-to-be?" I asked.

I remembered the girls who trained in Gion and Kyoto. From a very young age, they were taught to dance, sing, recite a poem, play the *shamisen*, pour tea, and satisfy men. But the women here were different. These women seemed to be wearing pale masks and behaved like walking puppets. I even noticed a sorrowful look behind the thick white face powder.

"Geishas only exist in Japan. We don't have geishas here," the man answered.

"So who are they?"

"They are comfort women. You'll understand when everything is settled."

When everything is settled.

My head was full of questions but my escort did not let me explore my curiosity. He introduced me to a middle-aged woman, who was Javanese and seemed to be the dormitory's matron.

They retreated into a corner and whispered to each other while now and then throwing a glance at me. Like the captain, she also nodded her head.

After the young man left, the woman asked me to choose a room. When I could not make up my mind, she picked the biggest one.

She took a deep bow as she closed the folding door. Once alone, I lay down on the neatly folded futon. It had been a tiring day and the sky was somber like the Chinese faces I had seen earlier.

Remembering the people, I sat up. Those dirty Chinese faces. Had I become like them?

I took a small mirror from my bag. I needed to look at my face to see if I had turned ragged like the Chinese at the harbor and in the dormitory.

My reflection appeared in the small mirror: a pointed chin, neat rows of pearly teeth, full lips, eyes as pretty as the sunlight on a warm spring day, and fair cheeks as soft as snow. Maybe I looked a little tired, but definitely not as harried as the dispirited Chinese.

Don't let anyone know you're Japanese.

*****

Shosho Kobayashi joined me a few days later. He was over fifty years old but had a glowing face and muscular body. He had a wife and three grown children in Japan—the oldest was already close to my age.

I met him at the nightclub in Kyoto where I worked as a geisha. He was one of our important guests. Yuriko-san asked me to serve and accompany Shosho Kobayashi.

"She is our best geisha," Yuriko-san said when introducing me.

Shosho Kobayashi was pleased with my service and asked for my company every time he visited. He gave me a lot of extra money, which fattened my savings.

I only knew he was one of Japan's lieutenant generals and held an important position. One evening at a tea ceremony with other generals, I heard talk of China, Singapore, Burma, and Thailand. They also mentioned Russia, Germany, England, and the Netherlands. Laughing, they raised their sake cups very high.

They boasted that tiny Japan, which Europe belittled, had easily devoured the giant Russian army in Manchuria. It was a great historical moment that showed the world Asians could no longer be underestimated. Japan emerged as an important country because of its triumph over Russia, and also as a symbol of Asia's victory over Europe. They made plans to enter other Asian countries. I had no idea if the Japanese would occupy them, but they would be considered the leader and under Japan's economic, political, and military control.

They also mentioned Indonesia, a country the Dutch colonized. Since the 1930s, many Japanese had migrated to Jakarta and Surabaya, opening stores or working as photographers. The generals thought Indonesia would soon belong to Japan.

I did not really understand what they said; my position as a geisha was only to serve Shosho Kobayashi.

He never talked very much. A Japanese woman was not allowed to know about a man's affairs. When Shosho Kobayashi finished his meeting, he asked me to bathe, massage, and serve him until he reached *yonaki,* his orgasm. He was like a general on the battlefield the way he was able to last. His strength was undiminished by his age.

I set foot on Java a year ago, when I was sixteen. I landed in Jakarta and stayed at Itsuka-san's place for several months before leaving for Surabaya.

Yuriko-san sent me with ten other girls from Gion to Jakarta. I was the only Japanese while the rest were young Chinese women whom our soldiers had taken away from their country after they conquered it.

"Shosho Kobayashi has been assigned to duty in Indonesia and he wants you to be with him. How do you feel about it?" Yuriko-san asked me while I was still in Japan.

I bowed my head, not giving her a reply. Life taught me that I did not need to give answers because He would make arrangements. Life was a skillful player—I had befriended Him when I was a child and knew He did not need any answer from me. Life would determine my fate.

I was a poor fisherman's daughter living on the outskirts of a city. My father and mother had ten children and I was the eighth and the youngest daughter. The first five were girls but my father wanted to have many boys to continue his family name, take care of his ashes when he and my mother had passed away, and help him to catch fish and inherit his battered boat to become fishermen themselves. Mother gave birth to five more children, all boys, except me—the eighth child.

Since I was the youngest daughter I should have been spoiled, but instead I was a burden to my parents. My older sisters and brothers helped Father search for fish. They sorted, carried, and salted the catch while I played on the beach building sand castles.

"I want to be the princess of this castle," I fantasized as a child. My brothers and sisters usually sneered and mocked me.

"You'll be the princess' maid," they said, and then roared with laughter while throwing the rotten fish they had picked out at me.

Only my mother cherished my dream. She said, "Someday you'll be a princess wearing a beautiful kimono because you are pretty."

My heart swelled when hearing my mother's compliment. I often dreamed I would turn into a beautiful princess in a bright silk kimono, with an attractive hair bun and nice smelling skin.

One day, mother called me. I was ten years old.

"Go with Takeshi-san," she said. "He will take you to Kyoto and send you to a school where you will learn to be a princess. You'll have pretty kimonos and always smell nice."

I was happy until I found out that my parents had sold me to Takeshi-san to lessen our poverty. One by one my older sisters and brothers grew up and married. My two youngest brothers were still too little to help catching fish, and I could not even push the boat or carry the fish. This meant I deserved to be sacrificed to lighten the family's burdens.

Takeshi-san took me to Kyoto, where I was sold to an *okiya*, a boarding house for geishas, and I worked as a *shikomi* or maid before I was enrolled at the geisha school in Gion.

The housemother of the okiya assigned me to Yuriko-san, one of Kyoto's most glamorous geishas. I served her as a personal shikomi for three years, cleaning her room and tatami, folding her futon mattress, cleaning her kimonos, and filling her ofuro for a hot bath. Everyday I watched her dress in one of her elegant kimonos, and comb her hair and tie it into a bun. I noticed her shiny ivory skin when she soaked in the warm water of the ofuro. She was my dream princess.

"Yuriko-san, you're gorgeous," I told her.

"You are, too. One day you'll be the most beguiling geisha. You have clear skin, an oval face, your eyes are not slanted like most Japanese, and your mouth is small and shapely." Yuriko-san tilted her head and continued while brushing the chalk-white paste on her face. "Your waist is small, your hips are rounded, and your breasts are full." Her eyes examined me from hair to toe through the mirror.

I could only blush.

During the years I served Yuriko-san, I cherished her beauty, her fragrance, her graceful movements and gentle ways, all of which turned her into a mesmerizing woman. I made up my mind to become a geisha who would at least be like her. I wanted to look pretty in colorful silk kimonos, my hair in a bun held together with exquisite hairpins, my face powdered, and wearing perfume. Everyone would look at me in admiration because I was the palace's princess.

East of Gion on Shijo Road was the Gion shrine I visited on my time off. I would bow twice before the gods, clasp my hands, and pray to be an enchanting geisha like Yuriko-san. I did not know if it was appropriate to say such a prayer. Perhaps I should have wished for something other than to be a geisha. However, from what I observed of Yuriko-san, a geisha was truly like being the princess I had dreamed of since I was little.

"In a few months you'll be enrolled at Gion's geisha school. You'll have the opportunity to learn a lot. First, you'll be a maiko," Yuriko-san said, smiling. "Study well—it's not easy to become a geisha. You not only have to be beautiful, but also smart, good at making men happy, and providing them with ultimate satisfaction," she ended, giggling.

Making men happy and giving them ultimate satisfaction—these words left a deep impression on me and kept ringing in my ears. They were the keywords of the training I received in Gion. I considered Yuriko-san my teacher since she had spoken these words first. I asked her many questions about the work to supplement my education—in my eyes she was truly a perfect geisha.

At the school, I learned how to wear the yukata, kimono, and obi. However, it was Yuriko-san who taught me how to match different colored obis and kimonos to create an attractive ensemble. The school taught me how to apply cosmetics and fix a hair bun, but it was Yuriko-san who gave me many ornate hairpins and bun-holders. I also learned to dance, sing, and play the shamisen, but it was Yuriko-san who taught me how to choose songs and read poetry with emotion. At school I also learned how to pour tea for the guests and entertain them during the *chanoyu*, or tea ceremony. However, it was Yuriko-san who taught me to perform the tradition with grace.

"When you pour tea, do so not only politely and following the rules, but also with grace and beauty. You must be able to pour tea while lifting up your sleeves inconspicuously, enabling the guest to peek into your kimono at least once since it covers your whole body. Also, the thick face powder prevents the guest from seeing your real face. Only when he has a glimpse of your underarm can he admire the beauty of your skin, which will later determine your price," she said.

That was Yuriko-san. The ten-year difference between us made her more of a mother than a peer, friend, or older sister.

I became a geisha when I was fourteen, after undergoing the *mizuage* to auction my virginity. Three rich and well-respected men in Kyoto bid on me. The housemother took me to them, and stripped off the layers of my obi and kimono until I stood naked.

The men looked like tigers ready to jump at their prey; their wild looks devoured my body.

Feeling uncomfortable, I moved my arms to cover my breasts, but the housemother jerked them back.

I was very surprised when my mizuage fetched the highest price among all the geishas of my graduation year in Gion. Yuriko-san said it was higher than hers.

"I told you already you'd be the most desired geisha, the most popular. I saw you grow up with an almost perfect body and face. Now you need to learn how to make men happy and give them ultimate satisfaction," she said, laughing heartily.

Indeed, I became one of the most popular geishas not only in Gion, but also in Kyoto. I was attractive, young, and fresh, and good at playing the shamisen, singing, reading poetry, making conversation, massaging, and making my guests reach yonaki. Glamorous kimonos and obis, glittering hair ornaments, face powder, and perfume made my appearance perfect. My childhood dream had come true.

At the peak of my fame as a geisha, Yuriko-san suggested I follow Shosho Kobayashi to Java. She said it was a golden opportunity I should seize since he had an important position there. If I joined him, I would also be an important woman. Besides, I heard that Surabaya and Jakarta were well-known ports where ships from many different countries such as the Netherlands, England, Portugal, and Japan docked. There were bound to be many entertainment places, and as Shosho Kobayashi's woman, I would receive special treatment.

At least I would not be just a geisha who had to compete with many others in Kyoto, and one day be removed because of old age. Being with Shosho Kobayashi meant I would only serve important guests with fat wallets.

I followed Yuriko-san's instructions. Shosho Kobayashi bought me from the housemother of the okiya, who in turn trusted Yuriko-san with a sum of money one could buy a house with. Yuriko-san organized everything for me, including my departure to Java.

"You're going with ten Chinese girls. Itsuka-san will take care of you when you arrive in Jakarta. You'll stay there until Shosho Kobayashi gives further instructions. He has left for important business in Surabaya.

"One thing to always remember: Itsuka-san may have changed your identity but you remain Japanese. We always return. No matter how dark the sky, Japanese seek the sun because the sun is life. As Japan represents the sun, Japan is life," Yuriko-san said when she saw me off.

"You must obey Shosho Kobayashi. Your duty is to serve him, make him happy, and provide him with ultimate satisfaction. He really likes you and bought you for a very high price. You are a very lucky geisha." Yuriko-san ended her farewell with, "May good fortune always be with you."

I diligently followed the arrangements Shosho Kobayashi had made. I stayed at Itsuka-san's shop in Jakarta for two months before moving to a big dormitory in Surabaya as Tjoa Kim Hwa.

Shosho Kobayashi took me to a *kurabu,* or club, owned by Hanada-san on Kembang Jepun, an area mostly populated by Chinese. Many were merchants but some ran the restaurants and clubs only rich people could afford.

Along Kembang Jepun stood the biggest, best, and most expensive clubs. The women were young, pretty, and carefully selected. Most were Chinese and Javanese. The Chinese were not like those who were kidnapped and sent from the war zones to Java, but women from cross-marriages between Chinese and Javanese priyayis. The Javanese women used to be Dutch mistresses. Only the women taken as spoils of war from Chinese, Korean, and Javanese villages were put into the kurabus.

"Just stay here until everything is fixed. Whatever happens, don't go anywhere. Everything will be all right. I'll come back for you," Shosho Kobayashi said when leaving me at the most expensive club on Kembang Jepun.

What did he mean by "until everything is fixed"?

*****

Black clouds rolled across a darkened sky in the misty morning. Heavy fog covered the sun—I wondered about the fog. It did not look like an ordinary morning fog that had not lifted. The fog looked more like billowing smoke, and the heavy columns rolled in from every direction to fill the sky.

Busy Kembang Jepun had turned quiet in the last few days. The Chinese shops, restaurants, and clubs were closed. No bicycle, ox cart, horse cab, or pedicab went by and neither did any of the Dutch soldiers who normally patrolled the street. The atmosphere was tense.

I heard a sudden commotion.

"*Fuse!*"

"*Hajime!*"

"*Atsumare!*"

Trumpets and whistles sounded one after another followed by the noise of artillery fire. Low flying planes and heavy armored tanks made the earth tremble. Explosions happened everywhere. The stink of cordite from gunpowder was strong and people screamed in panic. Dead bodies on the ground gave off the stench of blood. It was a frightening situation.

"What's going on? Why is there fighting?" I asked Hanada-san.

"Don't be scared. We'll be fine. Japan is bound to win."

"Are we at war?"

"Yes, with the Dutch." Hanada-san was calm, as if nothing had happened.

I could not help asking for more detail. "To occupy Indonesia?"

"To become the leader of Asia," he replied firmly.

I was stumped.

Hanada-san and I sat opposite each other at a short-legged table. A cup of sake absorbed the silence while murky light flickered in the lampion. The club's front door was tightly shut and the other women were in their rooms.

"Shosho Kobayashi has to take over the area between Kragan in Central Java and Surabaya in East Java. Besides him, other high-ranking Japanese officers are assigned to Palembang and West Java," Hanada-san volunteered.

"All the divisions are under the command of the 16th Army and Lieutenant General Hitoshi Imamura, who is responsible for Java and East Indonesia. Japan has also sent the 15th Army to Thailand and Burma, the 7th to Malaya, and the 14th to the Philippines. Our army, navy, and air force are insurmountable. We have captured the Kalijati

Airfield, which is forty kilometers from Bandung, and destroyed the planes of the Dutch and British troops. We have also entered Bandung, Jakarta, and Bogor. Last night I heard the 48th division has moved along three routes. The north route is going through Krangan–Lamongan–Gresik, the middle route through Krangan–Cepu–Bojonegoro–Nganjuk–Jombang–Mojokerto, and the south route through Blora–Cepu–Ngawi–Kertosono–Jombang. Surabaya is in our hands."

I was only a geisha and did not know about war strategy. My duty was to accompany the guests, make conversation, and listen to them although I did not understand what they talked about. This time the talk was interesting because it involved Shosho Kobayashi. My fate would be determined by these battles.

"Trust me. Soon the Dutch will retreat and Indonesia will be under our rule." Hanada-san smiled and swallowed his sake.

I poured more wine into his empty cup. "How can you be so sure?"

"We have studied the Dutch strengths, and the Japanese soldiers have the moral, political, and physical support from all Indonesian people. Indonesians don't like the Dutch. They like the Japanese better," Hanada-san replied.

"You've seen them in the Japanese shops. They're friendly to our people. They see Japan as an elder brother who will set them free from centuries of Dutch occupation. They expect a lot from us."

"Yes, Itsuka-san's shop in Jakarta was always busy with customers," I said.

"Do you know something? Itsuka-san is just like me. We, along with many others, entered Indonesia earlier disguised as shop owners, photographers, and restaurant owners. This enabled us to freely monitor the Dutch's military and economic strengths, as well as gauge the position of the Indonesians. The Dutch never suspected us to be military spies; the Japanese infiltrated this country before the actual confrontation. We gave the generals information so they could form plans to paralyze the Dutch easily. You don't believe it? See for yourself later."

I had to catch my breath. Now everything was becoming clear.

"By occupying Indonesia, Japan's economic and military position will be stronger in the eyes of Europe, and other Asian countries will fall under our control. Long live Japan! Long live the Emperor!" Hanada-san shouted as if victory was already won.

He swallowed his sake, refilled the cup, and drank again.

He sounded very cheerful and buoyant. It was as if he had grown wings out of his shoulders and could fly. He could become a dragonfly, a butterfly, or a bird. Or maybe even a combat plane. He laughed, shouted, and cheered, glorifying the Japanese troops he thought soon to be victorious, so great was his faith in them.

Unlike Hanada-san, I never felt sure. To me, life is not a matter of faith, since reality often differed from what

I wanted to believe. Life is not an exact science, either. I simply followed life wherever it took me.

Maybe my belief was different from the soldiers. They planned everything before making a move. As if life was in their hands, just like the fingers they used to count. One, two, three, and victory would definitely be theirs.

Definitely.

Certainly.

Is anything certain in life?

Within days, I heard the Dutch surrendered to Japan after a few easy battles. Their headquarters were bombed into ruins, their military bases and platoons mercilessly flattened. There was no room for negotiation, only orders to leave Indonesia immediately.

The Hinomaru flag flew over every part of Indonesia and people hailed the Japanese soldiers. Japan had really become this country's older brother, freeing the nation from the Dutch who had oppressed them for hundreds of years.

"Japan is the leader of Asia."

"Japan is the protector of Asia."

"Japan is the light of Asia."

The cheers followed the soldiers wherever they went. Indonesians regarded them as their nation's heroes.

Japanese soldiers arrested and disarmed Dutch soldiers. They were later imprisoned in the Kalisosok and Koblen prisons. Some were detained and interrogated in the Dutch Raad van Justitie building the Japanese had turned into the *Kempeitai,* or military police office. Soon the news spread by word of mouth that all day and deep into the night people on the street heard horrifying screams coming from the building.

Everyone knew the Japanese soldiers beat, punched, and kicked their Dutch prisoners, and also tortured them until they howled from the indescribable pain.

The Japanese put clamps on the prisoners' fingers, applied hot irons to their backs and chests, and ran electric current into their penises. Even the devil would not have been able to withstand their cruelty. Screams, whines, and howls from half-dead prisoners kept echoing and caused everyone passing the building to have goose bumps. One could not tell whether the screams came from a living human or a haunting ghost, but they definitely made a person's hair stand on end and run with wet pants. People soon named the Kempeitai, "the Ghost Building."

Big houses owned by Dutch people along Darmo Boulevard and the entertainment places they visited on Tunjungan Street were empty. Japanese soldiers confiscated all of them, and celebrated their victory at the clubs. They drank sake until they were tipsy and then looked for the warmth of a woman's body that could give them a new spirit. They scrambled to the kurabu dormitory on Ahmad Jais Street, where I stayed when I first arrived in Surabaya.

Japanese soldiers lustily overpowered the women. One woman had to serve ten to fifteen soldiers one after another because there were so many. The women did not receive payment or dared to ask for it. Instead of getting paid, they were spat on, shouted at, punched, had their hair pulled, and even trampled. There was no holiday or break. They even had to serve the soldiers during their menses.

One woman refused to have sex because she bled when urinating and it caused her pain. Her female organ discharged mucus that smelled as foul as a pile of rotten mice. With her body hot from fever and her face pale as death, she was unable to walk as all her bones felt as if they had been broken. She was unable to serve the men.

Instead of taking the woman to a doctor or giving her medicine, the soldiers took turns raping her. One soldier yanked her hair and punched her in the mouth. He forced her bloody mouth open to thrust his penis down into her throat. She tried to gag around the hardened organ but could not. He squirted his sperm and it burst out of her mouth with a gush of vomit.

She lay motionless in her spew, wet with tears, and crying without sound.

Another story I heard was that the soldiers entered women from the front and behind while lashing them with their belts until the bodies were covered with bruises. They were like cowboys riding their horses in a race, straddling up and down, forward and backward, while whipping the animals to make them run faster.

These sexual orgies were supposed to spur the soldiers to fight their enemies fiercely and mercilessly on the battlefield.

The kurabus were indeed meant for Japanese soldiers who were thirsty and hungry for a woman's body. The women could only cringe while they were subjected to the soldiers' raging lust. I also heard of Dutch women who gave themselves up so the soldiers would spare their husbands.

Liquor! Women! Victory!

I quivered when hearing the stories. I could not imagine anything I was told. No wonder I only saw spiritless murky faces, white as death without paint or powder, like grinning skulls. The women no longer smiled, as they were bodies without souls. All they did was spread their legs and provide a hole for the soldiers bursting with sexual urges. Like grenades, they exploded when hitting their target, ruining everything around them.

"They're not geishas," I sighed sadly.

I also served men to reach yonaki, but I did much more than just spread my thighs for tens of men to enter me. I could sing, play the shamisen, bathe my men in the ofuro, and make them fly high with a long moan.

I was a woman who artfully made love.

"They are not geishas, indeed," Hanada-san agreed.

"So what are they?" I really felt bad for their pain.

"We call them jugun ianfu, comfort women to satisfy a soldier's lust."

"Why so?"

"Because all soldiers need a woman. That's why you're here, too. Shosho Kobayashi needs one who is not a jugun ianfu. That's why no one must know you're Japanese. A Japanese woman can't be a jugun ianfu—that would be a disgrace. But you can't be a geisha either, as geishas only exist in Japan."

Now I understood everything that had confused me since I came to Indonesia.

"Everything is settled now," Hanada-san said.

"I'm Tjoa Kim Hwa, a Chinese woman," I mumbled, feeling unsettled.

Part 3: Matsumi

Surabaya 1942–1945

My heart carries too many hidden tears.

My lips were dry as I huddled weak, thirsty, and hungry in a corner of the deck. I had a gnawing pain in my stomach. My hair was unkempt, my face bruised, and my skin powdered with dust. As my heart cried out for Kaguya, I no longer cared for my body or face—all I thought about was my daughter.

I wished I could jump into the water and swim back to Surabaya. However, the ship had been sailing for weeks and the city had long disappeared from the horizon.

The sky grew darker, not only because the sun had gone to visit the night but also because rain clouds were coming in. The border between the sea and sky was hazy—I only saw a very thin line. It seemed life had vanished from the sea. The droning of the ship's engine competed with the sighs escaping from lungs dried by the salty air, and silence filled the moments between gusts ripping at the sails. A shrieking sea bird broke the silence. It flapped its wings and swooped down, gliding in the wind as it skimmed the waves. Only God knew where it was going.

The wind picked up and the waves became bigger. The ship swayed from side to side, rocking along with the raging sea, and my stomach started to churn. Raindrops fell on the ship and the people on deck looked for shelter, but there was none.

My face was wet from rain and tears.

My heart was heavy with sadness and doubt.

I had always followed the path Life showed me without ever questioning or turning from Him, but why did He keep dragging me into the dark corners?

Memories surged through my mind.

Life was an accomplished manipulator of time. Days passed by so quickly I didn't have a chance to take a breath. It only seemed like yesterday I was on a ship going to Surabaya and receiving special treatment from its captain. During that journey I did not lack anything and I had no reason to be scared.

Today I was on a ship under entirely different circumstances. Weary Chinese people looking for a better life did not surround me. Instead I was a hopeless, worn-out Chinese woman who desperately tried to catch a glimpse of the sun.

I was no different from the people I once pitied. In fact, at this time I could use some of their compassion. Hunkered in the corner of the deck without any possessions other than my breath and a slice of life thinner than paper, I had no idea where to go next. Life had stamped out my entire spirit although I was used to following Him and swallowing whatever He put in my mouth—things too hard to chew, always bitter on my tongue. I never had a choice. I was used to following where Life took me for lack of choices. Ever since I was a child, Life had presented me with hardships and challenges. Not once did He place something flavorful on my plate.

What about Kaguya? She was too young to be swept into Life's strong current and did not deserve to be subjected to His suffering. Had I become so worthless I could not fight for her life?

I held back my tears. Crying was useless. My heart already held too much sadness. After the Allies bombed Hiroshima and Nagasaki, the Emperor announced that Japan had surrendered. Many Japanese soldiers committed *seppuku,* ritual suicide, on hearing the news. Pilots and captains crashed their planes and warships into each other to blow themselves up and soldiers stabbed themselves with their swords. "Surrender" did not exist for them.

The circumstances in Indonesia became more uncertain. Before the Allied troops arrived, the Indonesian militia disarmed the remaining Japanese soldiers. News that the country would form a government and proclaim its independence quickly spread through the cities, villages, and countryside. The militia in every region, including Surabaya, immediately seized strategic points and government centers.

They ushered the Japanese soldiers to the Kalisosok and Koblen prisons, which became more crowded because of the Dutch soldiers already held there.

The nightclubs on Kembang Jepun were shut down. No one knew what happened to the kurabu on Ahmad Jais, except that hundreds of comfort women scrambled to freedom.

Japanese civilians were given the option to register and return to Japan by ship, or join the Homeland Defenders.

During a fierce battle between the Allies and the Japanese, Kaguya and I hid in the Boen Bio Temple on Kapasan Street, near my house. It seemed the Allies were set on getting even with the Japanese for the atrocities they committed during the war.

Troops arrived, guns were fired, grenades hurled, bombs exploded, and sirens blared.

The city was destroyed. Rice and farming fields were set on fire. Blood pooled in the streets. Dismembered corpses and injured bodies lay scattered around. War is a debasing madness that causes people to destroy each other.

People used the Boen Bio Temple as a refuge for its safety, and also because it was believed to have supernatural power. When the Japanese troops launched a massive attack on Surabaya and bombarded the city in 1942, two bombs fell on the rear of the temple but did not explode. It may have been a miracle. Since then, many people ran to the shrine to seek protection whenever there was a crisis.

The temple's caretakers did not mind providing asylum and food. The refugees were not only Chinese people who prayed in the temple, but also Javanese who lived in the surrounding neighborhood.

Kaguya and I were the only Japanese.

At first, no one knew. My skin was fair and my eyes were slanted while Kaguya looked like an Indonesian girl with her big round eyes and curly eyelashes. It was only her fair olive skin that made her different from native children.

I also could read the Chinese letters in the temple; except for the pronunciation, they were very similar to kanji. I also joined in the rituals because they were similar to those I practiced as a child in Japan.

However, we could not stay long because Kaguya spoke neither Javanese nor Chinese. We talked in Japanese. The other refugees noticed and started a rumor about my nationality.

A man from the temple asked me to come to his office. "I'm one of the caretakers. People call me Tuan Tan," he said.

"I'm Tjoa Kim Hwa."

Tuan Tan continued to speak in Chinese and I started to tremble. While I knew what he said, I did not understand his question precisely. He seemed suspicious of my identity and I was overcome by fear.

Was he going to send me away? Where could I go with my two-year-old in the war-torn city? I panicked and wriggled in my chair as if I was sitting on a bed of hot coals.

When I did not answer his question, Tuan Tan gave me a piercing look.

"You're Japanese," he mumbled.

"Yes, but I speak a little Indonesian," I stammered. "I can read kanji, too."

"Why are you hiding here?" Tuan Tan asked in Chinese. He grabbed a white piece of paper, wrote several letters on it, and passed it to me.

I read what he had written and jotted my answer: Am I not allowed?

Tuan Tan looked at me, perplexed. He wrote: Where do you live? Why did you come to this temple? The Chinese hate the Japanese. Their soldiers slaughtered three hundred thousand people in Nanking. They are very cruel, and they treated the Indonesians even worse. To Indonesians, the Japanese are nothing but liars. They said Japan would help Indonesia regain sovereignty, but they made us suffer even more than under Dutch rule. Romusha, jugun ianfus, poverty, fear, and oppression were all the Japanese brought to Indonesia. Why don't you join your people's evacuation?

He meticulously wrote out his reservations: How did you end up here? No other Japanese woman ever came here. What will happen if Indonesian militia found you here?

He fastened an inquisitive look on me.

I remained quiet, with tears gathering at the corners of my eyes. It was difficult to start the story. My tongue stiffened, and I was numb. The fear of having no place to go was agonizing. I gasped, no longer able to hold back my tears.

Japanese people are gathering and registering to be sent back to Japan. Don't you want to join them? Tuan Tan wrote.

"Yes, I'd like to," I replied, trembling.

Tuan Tan waited for me to continue.

I hesitated. Was he a kind man, or did he harbor a grudge against Japanese people? Would he report me to the militia? What should I do? Could I trust him? I was confused.

"What do you think?" Tuan Tan urged me to respond. His fatherly voice erased my suspicions. I had no choice but to tell him my story and place Kaguya's fate and mine in his hands. I prayed he would feel pity for us.

"Yes, I'd like to," I said. "But my daughter would not be accepted."

Tuan Tan frowned.

Why can't she return with you? he wrote again.

We took turns writing responses to each other—She's Indonesian. Her father is Javanese—I finally rolled the enormous burden off my back.

Tuan Tan was dumbfounded. After a while he resumed his questions: Who's her father? A regent? A vice regent? A rich man? Where does he live? I'll take you to his home. You'll be safe and won't need our refuge.

His sincere kindness touched the deepest part of my heart. Not all Chinese people hated the Japanese. Shaking my head, I burst into tears.

I don't want to see my daughter's father, I wrote with tears staining my face. I want to move as far away from him as possible. I never want to see him.

I covered my face with my hands and wept. Tears seeped between my fingers while my shoulders shook.

My unceasing sobs and moans were the only sound in the temple. Tuan Tan did not try to stop me. He gave me time to release the sadness I had always kept to myself.

He wrote: Cry, if that makes you feel better. Ever since the war broke out, we have not been able to stop crying. You can cry as much as you want. Don't worry—you're safe here. Once you feel better, you can tell me your story. I'll listen. Hopefully I'll be able to help.

My sobbing quieted as the fear, anxiety, anger, and sadness that raged uncontrollably inside me at last subsided. I took a very deep breath to fill the void in my chest that had been there a long time.

Tuan Tan poured a cup of steaming hot tea. The aroma blended with the fragrance of burning incense sticks seeping into the office and created a mystical atmosphere. He gave me time to calm myself. "Here, drink this. It will make you feel better and warm you."

I took the cup with trembling hands, blew on the hot drink, and sipped slowly. Its warmth spread from my throat and chest to my stomach. Tuan Tan was right—the tea was soothing. His presence was also a comfort. I felt more at ease and decided to trust him. After heaving a long sigh, I started to write again.

On hearing we would be returned to Japan, I knew that I should not waste the opportunity. It did not matter whether Japan had won or lost. I had to return to my homeland.

Many people were dead after the destruction of Hiroshima and Nagasaki, and the trades and industries were paralyzed. But Japan was my country. I could live there with Kaguya, my daughter, regardless of any chaos.

I had to take her because she was my most valuable possession. Nothing could make me stay in Surabaya. I had to move far away without ever looking back.

More precisely, I wanted to leave Sujono.

But I could not take Kaguya because she did not have any identification documents. The Indonesian militia would not permit her to leave and the Japanese would refuse her entry. She was Sujono's child, illegitimate from my relationship with a Javanese man.

"Who is he?" Tuan Tan asked.

Sujono. Something pierced my heart whenever I remembered the name.

He had turned my life upside down. Although I used to be deeply in love with him, I hated him now. While I had put my trust in him at first, I ended up eliminating him from my life. I once sacrificed everything for him.

I knew Sujono as a very romantic man, which made him intoxicating. He worked as a coolie at Babah Oen's shop, the biggest shop on Coklat Street. I often saw him bare-chested and heaving bolts of cloth onto a pedicab. His chest was thin but strong; his skin was very dark and perspiration made it glisten under the sun. There was nothing special about him. He was not even attractive. I noticed him because he often made eyes at me. He stopped at Hanada-san's club on Kembang Jepun to drop off the fabric ordered by the women. Every time Sujono appeared, he searched for me out of the corners of his eyes, and threw me affectionate looks when he found me. He usually sat in the back and smoked to kill the time.

The back of the club was closed off. Private rooms and an ofuro were located there while the front was used for guests. This area was furnished with short-legged tables and tatami mats to sit on. There was also a small stage for dance performance and playing the shamisen. A small corridor led to the ofuro and row of rooms to serve the guests.

I often saw Sujono sitting at the back. He stayed in the club after delivering the order. Smoking, he observed me as I brought a guest to the ofuro and escorted him to my room.

Hanada-san's club was known as one visited by dignitaries like Shosho Kobayashi, who was very influential in Surabaya. The club was also famous for its beautiful young women. I was one among them.

People knew me as Tjoa Kim Hwa, the Golden Flower Snake.

Once I established myself as the top hostess, my rates increased. I carefully picked the guests I spent time with. I drank sake with ordinary guests, sang and played the shamisen for them, but I gave extra service to the important ones referred by Shosho Kobayashi. And of course, I received extra payment. Yuriko-san's advice was deeply entrenched in my mind—make them happy and give them ultimate satisfaction.

From the first time I became a geisha, I applied everything I learned at the school in Gion and from Yuriko-san to make men happy. This gave me greater income.

But one thing I never did was to kiss a guest on the lips. Yuriko-san once said, "A geisha's duty is to entertain—she is not to involve her emotions. Only kiss the man you love."

After enjoying sake, conversation, and singing, I usually offered the important guest a bath in the ofuro. While he soaked in the warm water, I rubbed, or more precisely rubbed and caressed, his back and chest with a washcloth. After this I helped him put on a clean kimono and escorted him to a room. There I took off his kimono and undressed as well. With the grace of a dancer I peeled off my clothes layer by layer. Naked, I gently massaged and caressed him.

I started by massaging his back, then his neck, chest, and the rest of his body. While massaging, I brushed my nude body against his. Slowly but surely, his skin warmed and his breath started to puff like a locomotive. I continued leading the play until he reached yonaki.

Yes, I made men happy.

I knew how to guide them to yonaki.

I always followed what Yuriko-san told me when I served a guest.

Did I? My eyes burned and a sharp pain filled my chest.

Since meeting Sujono, I no longer paid attention to Yuriko-san's lessons. Sujono changed my life. He gave me joy, but also grief when he turned my life upside down.

I started to chat with him because I didn't have anyone else at Hanada-san's club. The guests who bought my service were not interested in a genuine conversation. All the women at the club were jealous of each other, especially me because I received preferential treatment from Shosho Kobayashi and Hanada-san. They suspected me of being Japanese. However, they couldn't prove it as everyone at the club had to speak Japanese and wear a kimono.

"I'm actually Japanese," I admitted to Sujono. "My true name is Matsumi. Tjoa Kim Hwa is the name given to me when I was smuggled into this country. It is an absolute disgrace for a Japanese woman to work as a hostess in a foreign country. Japanese men don't want to disgrace their own women in a foreign country."

It happened naturally. I started to trust Sujono, and from him I learned to speak simple Indonesian. I had kept my true identity a secret until I revealed it to him. I needed someone I could talk to without fear. Before I kept this feeling to myself. As long as Shosho Kobayashi was there, life at the club remained easy and safe for me. But I felt so restless that I became afraid.

Who could bear such feelings alone?

"Do you like your job?" Sujono asked while making a delivery and Hanada-san was not at the club.

"I've been a geisha since I was fourteen."

"That's not what I asked," he snapped. "Do you like your job?"

"Why? What's wrong with being a geisha?"

"Do you know what kind of work you're doing?"

"I'm an artist."

He burst into laughter.

"It's not easy to be a geisha." I tried to explain because his laughter offended me. "We go through a lot of training and learn to sing, dance, play the shamisen, recite poetry, and entertain our guests with a tea ceremony."

"And entertain your guests in the bedroom," he added.

I resented the demeaning tone of his remark.

"In this country, your job is the most despicable one could ever have."

"How come?" I could not accept his statement. It took me years to become a geisha, and all of a sudden the profession was considered something very low in Indonesia.

"Have you heard of the women in the kurabu?" Sujono asked.

I nodded.

"Have you heard their stories?"

I nodded again.

"What's the difference between you and those women?"

I could only be quiet.

"The difference is they are used to satisfy the lust of any Japanese soldier, but you only serve the high-ranking officers. The difference is the kurabu women are not paid, but men pay you a lot of money."

How dare he be so rude? Had I sunk that low in the eyes of this textile shop coolie? I felt humiliated.

He continued his string of hurtful words. "The Japanese do not want to disgrace their women so they asked you to pretend to be Chinese. Do they think about the dignity of women from other nations? Chinese and Korean women are brought by force to Japan, Indonesia, and any other place to serve the lust of Japanese soldiers. Now they're taking Indonesian women. Don't you realize how cruel the Japanese are?"

I wanted to be angry, but I couldn't. Deep inside where my restlessness and fear resided, I only could agree.

Being a woman, I often wept when hearing stories about the jugun ianfu in the kurabus. Whether Javanese, Chinese, or Korean, they were women like me. Only they were forced to serve men under threats. It was shameful and inappropriate I took pride in my status at the most expensive club in Kembang Jepun.

"How much would I have to pay to get the service you provide for your guests?" Sujono asked.

Dumbfounded, I was unable to answer. How could I tell him that he couldn't afford Hanada-san's cheapest courtesan with his coolie income, let alone me?

Since that time, Sujono was heavy on my mind. His stealthy looks and body odor mixed with the scent of his cigarette haunted me, until one day Hanada-san told me I had an unusual guest requesting my service. And the guest was Sujono.

"Where did you get the money?" I asked in the bedroom.

"None of your business. What's most important is that I can pay for you. I want to know how you make a man happy."

He was correct. It was my duty to satisfy him since he had paid for my services. But I felt like an ant under an elephant's foot and could not perform as I did for my usual guests.

Sujono fixed his eyes on me and took off my clothes. This surprised me and made my heart pound. We stood so close to each other I could smell his body and breath. I closed my eyes as his hands slithered over my body like snakes. I quivered while holding back my arousal, something I never had with other guests. I was the one who gave pleasure and controlled the play. But he engulfed my body and I no longer had control. Swept by the torrent of passion, I was unable to contain my groans and whimpers. When we finished and I languished in absolute contentment, his lips closed over my mouth. His tongue explored mine and I savored the sweet taste of his cigarette.

We were kissing.

I involved my feelings in my relationship with Sujono. He changed my world. He adored me, loved me, and wanted to have me. He bewitched me.

Sujono was like sake—sweet, intoxicating, and making me fly. He was a dream.

Even as a geisha, I never knew what falling in love, loving, or being loved felt like. No man had flattered me. My duty was to satisfy every man who slept with me, and this obligation was firm in my heart and mind. The more guests I satisfied, the higher my rate.

Sujono introduced me to a new world, one I never knew in my life as a geisha.

He was a seducer, romantic and passionate. He was like fire. He made me feel I was a woman. He made me fall in love.

"Matsumi, you're like a princess. You're beautiful, gentle, and desirable. I'll never let you leave me. I want you to be mine," he told me every day after showering me with his fiery kisses.

He not only worshipped me with words as sweet as honey, but also made me relish the sensations he created when he touched every part of my body. He was wild, fierce, and lustful—very different from my guests, older men with big stomachs and rolls of sagging fat; who were slow and had difficulty moving; who lay on their backs and gave orders for what they needed to reach yonaki.

Sujono made me feel seductive. He touched me like an artist sculpting a statue and caressed me like a painter stroking his brush on a piece of paper. He was a poet writing his poems on every part of my skin.

His attention made him a great lover. He embraced, caressed, kissed, and grappled with me in the clouds, on the crest of rolling waves driven by the wind. It was like the moon making love with the night, like the sun courting the light. We breathed, drenched in perspiration, passion escaping from the pores of my skin. He was intoxicating.

Erotic. Irrational. He made me float, until one day I said to him, "I'm pregnant."

Sujono was excited. He immediately pulled me into a tight embrace and covered me with kisses.

"Great! I'll have a daughter as lovely as an angel."

Never in history had a geisha become pregnant and given birth. When geishas grew old, younger ones automatically replaced them. Or they retired by choosing a *danna*—a wealthy man who, like a husband, would support all their needs. I could not give birth while being a geisha. Worse still, I was in Surabaya, a city I was unfamiliar with.

"It's impossible," I said.

"Why?" Sujono interrupted me.

"Geishas never have children."

"I actually don't want you to be a geisha."

"But this is my profession."

"Be my wife. You'll be mine."

Oh, how wonderful that sounded.

If it was a dream, I did not want to wake up. I wanted to sleep and live the dream forever. Could there be anything more perfect than belonging to someone who loves you and you love?

I wanted to be with Sujono and forever serve him with all my heart and love. I did not expect anything in return. I would pour his tea, sing, and play the shamisen for him. We'd make orisurus, together and imagine the paper cranes flying toward the sunrise or sunset. And at night we'd slip onto the futon to make love and sleep in each other's arms until the morning.

In my imagination I pictured a little house where we lived happily after I gave birth to the child I carried. In the morning, Sujono went to work while I waited for him and took care of our child. In the evening, we played with the baby. Although we lived modestly, our happiness and love by far outweighed the simple life. Wasn't this a wonderful dream?

The dream made me a complete woman.

Loving and being loved, serving and being served, and sharing life are the dream of every woman on this earth.

What I wished for was by no means impossible. It was a very simple desire.

Hanada-san tried to prevent me from leaving the club. He did not only have the club's interest at heart, but since we were both Japanese, he was also concerned for my safety.

"Matsumi, please stay. If you want to go, I'll ask Shosho Kobayashi to help you return to Kyoto."

"No. I like it here. I plan to stay for good." This was the only time I made my own decision. I had always let destiny control my life, and never argued or said no. It felt magical to say no.

Finally I decided to tell Hanada-san the truth.

"I have to go with Sujono. I'm pregnant with his child."

Hanada-san's slanted eyes widened until they seemed ready to fall out of their sockets. He gasped, opening and closing his mouth several times without uttering a sound. His facial expression showed anger and disappointment.

"*Nan desu ka,* really?" he hissed.

"Yes. *Gomen nasai,* I'm sorry." All I could do was bow as deeply as possible.

"Matsumi, how could you let this happen?" Hanada-san shouted, staring at me in disbelief.

He slapped me so hard that I staggered. My cheek burning, I bowed as deep as I could. I knew I had committed a grave mistake.

"Did you forget that you're the most popular geisha? No geisha has ever gotten pregnant. As a hostess, she must maintain the beauty of her face and body. Pregnancy and birth will cause damage to both."

"I'm quitting. Sujono will not allow me to work as a geisha."

"Matsumi!" Hanada-san yelled. "You're out of your mind. I don't understand what you're thinking."

"I'll be Sujono's wife and the mother of his child."

"*Bakayaro,* you're a fool. If you want a husband, you can find a man far better than Sujono, someone who'd give you a house and provide security. You wouldn't need to work as a geisha anymore, just make one man happy and serve him.

"What can you expect from Sujono? He's a textile shop coolie. How can he meet your needs? He has to work up a sweat just to meet his own needs, never mind supporting you. Use your brain, Matsumi."

Hanada-san only knew Sujono as an errand boy for Babah Oen's textile shop, which several women in his club patronized. When he happened to be in a good mood, he'd tip Sujono a few cents. He never expected me to fall in love with a coolie.

Sujono had once paid for my service, and to Hanada-san money was everything. As long as a man paid my fee, it did not matter who he was. Hanada-san did not know that Sujono only paid for me the first time. Afterward he paid with money I gave him.

But it was a different matter to Hanada-san now that I was in love and wanted to be Sujono's wife. He was my patron and responsible for my welfare. Besides, Shosho Kobayashi had to be taken into consideration. Hanada-san was right; it would not be difficult for me to find a danna, or ask to be returned to Japan if I did not want to be a geisha anymore. However, being in love and getting pregnant with a poor local man was not an option.

"I'm sorry, but I love Sujono," was all I could say. I kept bowing deeply, not daring to look into Hanada-san's eyes. I knew I had committed a serious offense.

"Love does not exist for a geisha. She is an exquisite porcelain doll that cannot crack. Love causes the porcelain not only to crack but also shatter into pieces. You don't know your place. You're ungrateful. You don't know how to return a favor. You're only capable of ruining your own life and future. Stupid woman! Bitch! Bakayaro!"

Hanada-san slapped my face over and over while he cursed me. My face was swollen and burned from his slaps but I did not shed any tears. The pain I felt was like an ant's bite in comparison to the loneliness I had suffered for years. Why should I cry?

"I'm sorry," I said again and again.

I allowed Hanada-san to take his anger out on me as much as he liked. Not only did he slap me, he also pulled my hair, kicked me, and punched my head. After he finished his chastising he glared at me with an expression I did not understand. "Go," he said, with a voice so cold it made my teeth clatter. "Never come back."

He spat at my face and left without looking back at me.

I dragged my feet across the floor but did not cry.

Tuan Tan took a long drag of his pipe. He did not interrupt me as I wrote, but nodded when he finished reading what I had written on the paper.

Do you love Sujono that much? he wrote.

I used to. Not anymore. I regret ever having loved him.

Why do you regret? You sacrificed so much for him.

He's not the right man.

Is he a good person?

I don't know.

What do you mean?

I don't know if he is good or not. He loves me a lot. He loves me very much. But he loves me in his own way, which I think is not quite right.

"How so?" Tuan Tan asked out loud, and waited for my reply.

Stillness settled on the windowsill as twilight began to fall and the shrine's candles cast shadows in the office.

I wrote out more of my story.

Finally I left Hanada-san's club on Kembang Jepun. With my savings I bought a house from a Chinese person. It was not too big or too small; it was just the right size for

Sujono, our child after it was born, and me. I also looked for a maid.

In that house I entrusted my hopes for the future to Sujono. I knew he already had a wife and a son, but that did not matter to me. Many geishas had a danna who was already married and had children. It did not mean I would be Sujono's second wife. I did not give that any consideration. I just wanted to be with him.

I always served him with all my heart, not only on the futon but also in everything else. I devoted myself to him in the way a Japanese woman reveres her man. Although we had a maid, I served him. He was such a warm and intoxicating man and showered me with so much passion and affection that I was willing to do anything for him.

Everyday he spent his time adoring and caressing me and being jealous. He did not care about his work as long as he could be by my side, making love all the time.

"I can work anytime. Many Chinese shops other than Babah Oen's need coolies, but nothing can replace being with you," he said. "Working makes me tired and bored. But making love with you is always tender and enjoyable. I can't think of anything else but you," he told me.

"Matsumi, I have suffered so much. For years I worked as a coolie for wages only enough for cigarettes. Now I must feed my wife and her son. Why can't I enjoy life a little bit? Being with you makes me forget all the problems that spout from Sulis's mouth."

My savings had dwindled, as they were all we had to live on while I got bigger with my pregnancy. I wanted to work but did not know what I could do. I had never done anything except be a geisha and my skills were only singing, reciting poetry, playing the shamisen, dressing attractively, and serving guests. No club would employ a pregnant woman, and I could not run a *warung* like many Javanese women or work for a Chinese shop.

Anyway, it was Sujono who should find work.

But he did not want a permanent job. He worked when he felt like it and his wages were never enough to support his wife and son, even for a very simple life. Still, he did not seem to care much about work.

Sujono always returned to his home after we made love. That was not all. He became financially dependent on me for meeting the needs of his family. He did not have any sense of responsibility toward his work. As time went by, I could no longer deceive myself. I realized that one could not live from only love and passion.

All Sujono wanted from me was money and sexual pleasure.

He was taking advantage of me.

He was no longer a lover.

That was not fair. I was trapped between the spokes of a rolling wheel. I could not go backward but I also found it difficult to move forward.

Sujono loved me in his own unique way. He not only shattered my dreams but also trampled my self-respect. He chained me and I did not know how to free myself.

His love made me very tired as he had countless rules that justified his talking and jealousy. He did not allow me to wear nice clothes or put on face powder and lip rouge. He even prohibited me from smiling and looking at a man.

His jealousy was crazy.

"You're no longer Golden Flower, you're my wife. You're old and pregnant, and your body is not as desirable like before. Men don't want you, even when you seduce them with your eyes," he chuckled cynically and threw me a look filled with jealousy.

"Remember not to leave the house without me. No one knows that you're Japanese. Everyone thinks you're Chinese. Everyone hates the Japanese because they are cruel liars. In the villages, people cannot eat because Japanese soldiers confiscated their rice. Many husbands and sons have died as romushas. Girls hide because they're scared of being forced to become jugun ianfu. Even if the soldiers don't take them away, they rape them where they are. If people find out you're Japanese, they'll strip you and parade you naked as revenge. It will be worse if they know you've worked in a club on Kembang Jepun. To the Indonesians, you're nothing but a prostitute, a whore, a slut."

Was that a form of love?

If it was, Sujono's love was insulting and made me feel worthless. I felt helpless, and physically and emotionally exhausted. The days were very long, filled with financial problems and endless fights triggered by his outrageous jealousy. He hurt me deeply with mockeries that shot out of his mouth like missiles.

His words always hurt.

So did his wild sexual desire.

He no longer treated me like his sweetheart, but worse than he'd treat a geisha, jugun ianfu, prostitute, whore, slut, or any other word he used in his cursing.

He was rough when sleeping with me, regarding his strength as proof of his virility. He demanded that I meet his physical needs the way he saw fit almost everyday. He spread my thighs and lifted and folded them. He kneaded and rolled me as if making sushi and treated my body like a piece of paper, making me into anything he wanted. I found no satisfaction in our union. Sujono made lovemaking lose its beauty, tenderness, and even passion. He disgusted me, leaving my whole body and my heart in pain.

I could no longer get through the nights without tears. Reality turned out to be entirely different from my dreams. I felt like a ship stranded on a poisonous island without a captain, wind direction, or lighthouse.

With the help of a midwife, I gave birth to my daughter just before sunrise. All night long I had groaned in pain only accompanied by the maid—Sujono had gone to his own home. The twisting pain was as though my bones were being broken. How sad it was to give birth without a husband at my side. When I felt wet at the corners of my eyes, I did not know if the tears were caused by physical or emotional agony.

Fluid gushed between my thighs; I felt something tear and heard a sound. My baby left my body crying.

Then the sun rose.

My baby was as radiant as the first rays of the sun. Her skin was as soft as the snow on Mount Fujiyama, and her round clear eyes framed by thick dark eyebrows resembled those of a Javanese princess. I named her Kaguya.

"In the Japanese folktale, Kaguya is an angel who changed into a human," I told Sujono.

I wished that my daughter would grow into an angel blessed with supernatural powers, and turn all that is ugly into something lovely with a simple chant. Maybe Kaguya's presence would make my life enjoyable again. I wanted her fate to be as beautiful as her face, and life to treat her kindly. My fate did not match my face.

After giving birth, I told Sujono I wanted to work at Hanada-san's club if he'd accept me, or at another club on Kembang Jepun because not much money was left. I did not know what else to do in Surabaya.

"Go back to prostitution, whoring, and being a slut? No way," he said firmly, his lips pressed in a straight line. "You're mine, and only mine. I don't want other men to see or touch you. Besides, you're old. You have a child and your face and body are no longer young and tempting. No club would accept you as a hostess. The only thing you might be good for is a jugun ianfu in the kurabu house," he said cynically.

"I'm a geisha," I replied, feeling hurt.

I never felt like a prostitute, a whore, or a slut. I was a geisha. It was not easy to become one. I did not just lie down on my back and open my legs for a man. I studied many years. I was trained to accompany guests, engage them in conversation, and pour tea for the tea ceremony. I learned to recite poetry, sing, and play several musical instruments.

If at the end of the evening we headed for the bed, I was taught how to take off my kimono gracefully, and massage and caress my guest to yonaki.

"What's the difference between a geisha and a jugun ianfu? Both sleep with many men." Sujono's hurtful words pierced my heart.

I did not know if he meant it as an insult, abuse, or an expression of jealousy, but whatever it was, he damaged my pride. I was indeed a geisha, a hostess, and an artist. I enjoyed my life because I lived as a princess in my sand castle.

When Sujono came to my castle, he knew the kind of life I had; it was comfortable and glamorous, yet fragile. My castle was beautiful but easily ruined when the waves swept over it. A geisha held on to her fame until her twenties, when a younger one replaced her. Then a geisha needed a danna to support her for the remainder of her life.

But I had left my castle because I fell in love with a man I thought would give me perfect love. I was willing to exchange my sand castle for a simple but strong house. I was not concerned about large sums of money I could earn easily, and refused to seek a danna because I wanted to surrender my life and future to Sujono.

What did I get?

He made me leave Kembang Jepun that showered me with luxuries, and walk toward a future that had no certainty.

The dream was short. When I came to my senses, I found he was no more than a snake.

He was venomous.

He was bitter.

He was toxic.

He was poisonous.

He was scum.

His sweetness turned toxic when he could not provide us with food. His charm became venom when our mouths were dry from thirst, his love turned into chains without ends, and his dreams became a typhoon that ruined hopes for the future.

Sujono only gave me the inebriating sweetness for several months. When the honey dried up only bitterness was left in my mouth. He did not have a permanent job and our living expenses were high. He also asked me for money to support him. My savings were shrinking fast; I had not worked since I left Hanada-san. Also, Kaguya was born.

He hurt me.

I really hated him.

My tears stained my cheeks after I unloaded my burden. Everything moved like silhouettes through my mind: My poverty-stricken childhood on the coast, the beautiful city of Gion, Yuriko-san who was kind, becoming a geisha, beauty, youth, fame, beautiful kimonos and fragrant powder, the aroma of sake, plucking the shamisen, the shower of luxuries, the trip to Surabaya, working at Kembang Jepun, Sujono, and Kaguya.

"Oh, I see," Tuan Tan said when I finished.

I want to go away as far as possible. I don't want to see him anymore, I repeated to myself. I must return to Japan because a Japanese person must return. There is the sun and the sun is life, I copied Yuriko's words. Kaguya and I will have a better life. But I'm confused and desperate. I don't know what to do since I changed my identity when I entered Indonesia. There is no document for Matsumi, only Tjoa Kim Hwa. I'm registered as Chinese, not Japanese. Worse, Kaguya doesn't have any papers. I can't take her with me.

I choked as I wrote and was overcome by despair when I finished. I screamed like a mad woman until I calmed myself and was able to hold the pen once again.

*****

When I heard the Japanese surrendered, I went to Hanada-san's club in Kembang Jepun before I went to this temple despite the fact he had sent me away. I didn't know where else to go. I wanted to ask for his help but the club had been shut down. Many Indonesian militia soldiers patrolled the street up to Jembatan Merah. No one could enter or exit the area. Later I learned that Hanada-san was detained in the Kalisosok prison when his identity as a Japanese spy was uncovered. The club had only served as camouflage.

It was impossible to go to the prison and look for him. There were thousands of Japanese people inside. Still, I wouldn't have dared tell them I was Japanese. I also went to the Kempeitai building to find Shosho Kobayashi, even though I expected him to hate me because I had left the club. For all I knew, he might even kill me. I was ready to receive his punishment. I just wanted to ask his help with returning to Japan with Kaguya. If he could smuggle me into Indonesia as Chinese, he must be able to send me to Japan as Japanese. He knew my true identity.

When I arrived at the Kempeitai office, Shosho Kobayashi and his soldiers looked grief stricken instead of angry and determined. They had expressions of dull acceptance on their faces.

Shosho Kobayashi was not mad at me. "Why did the Emperor willingly surrender to the Allies? Japan never gives up. All of us are ready to fight for him and our country's greatness. Although Hiroshima and Nagasaki were burned to ashes, we should have never surrendered, not even if the Allies had bombed the whole country. We never fear death. If we have to choose between defeat and death, we choose death. Defeat is shameful. We'd rather die."

Tears streamed from his eyes, but a Japanese soldier does not know how to cry. He put his gun, hat, and military decorations on the table. He kneeled down, took out his samurai sword, and shouted, "For the Emperor and Japan! We are never defeated!" He stabbed the sword deep into his belly and twisted it until his entrails fell out. His blood flowed over the handle of the sword he clutched and his body fell to the ground. He died before my eyes.

I continued writing with trembling fingers.

Seeing him commit seppuku, the soldiers knelt one by one to pay respect to his dead body. They took off their hats and bowed their heads. They sang "Kimigayo" sorrowfully, but without shedding tears. They were accustomed to death and it was honorable to die like him—he died a hero. To them, defeat was more terrifying than death.

After honoring Shosho Kobayashi's body, the soldiers took out their revolvers. Some put them against their forehead and others into their mouths. They pulled the triggers; the guns exploded.

The bodies immediately fell with bulging eyes and blood splashed on the floor, tables, chairs, walls, windows and me. Everyone was dead; no one was left. An eerie stillness enveloped the building. The pillars still stood proud and strong; I only heard my own breathing. I trembled at seeing so many bodies. I was the only one alive amid the smell of death.

I couldn't cry, scream, or make any sound. I didn't know who to look for, or where I should go. My mind went blank.

I was exhausted after writing my story. My whole body felt faint, as if every joint had loosened. The treadmill of life had sapped all my energy. "I should have chosen death, too. I'm very scared," I said in halting Indonesian. The voice came from another world, not from my mouth and tongue. It was the voice of my heart.

Tuan Tan was stunned after reading my story.

He wrote: Wherever they are fought, wars always leave grief, wounds that never heal. Time may help grow a scab, but the scars are always there. No one is right or wrong in a war. People simply kill each other. War doesn't give anything but pain.

You'll be safe here as long as people don't know you're Japanese. If someone tells the Indonesian militia, they might raid our temple. We can't count on everyone to be quiet about your presence. You know the Indonesians and Chinese don't like your people. If someone reports you, I can't guarantee your safety.

I gasped. My chest felt like it was going to burst. I bowed my head and stared at the dust on the floor.

Tuan Tan was right. Although I did not hear any rejection in his explanation, I understood the difficulty of my situation.

He continued his turn with the pen: Our temple only serves as a shelter until the situation outside improves. I hear the Indonesian radicals are ready to proclaim the country's independence. There will be a new nation. I don't know what happens once the new government has rearranged everything, but it won't be something you'll like.

If I may advise you, it's best to return to Japan now. You won't be alone. Thousands of Japanese are being shipped to their homeland. This opportunity won't come twice. I have no idea what the new government will do to your people in Indonesia once they take control. Will they imprison or punish them? I don't know.

Tuan Tan shook his head.

I was only concerned about Kaguya. My breath depended on her laughter and crying; she was my life and soul. I would do anything to save her. Despite the difficulties, I carried on because of her. My desire to leave Surabaya and Sujono was not because I was giving up. On the contrary: I wanted a better life for Kaguya, to take her to Japan and far from Sujono. I was certain a good life waited for us in Japan.

"In my opinion, you should leave her with her father. What's his name? Hmm, yes, Sujono."

"Oh, no. That wouldn't be good," I managed in Indonesian.

"But he's her father. He'd take care of her. Your daughter would be safe in Indonesia," Tuan Tan said slowly.

"You're right about her safety here but wrong about leaving her with Sujono," I stammered, trying to express myself in Indonesian.

"He loves you so much. He'd surely love Kaguya."

"Yes, but he's not the right man."

"What do you mean?"

"He doesn't have a permanent job." I halted and reached for a sheet of paper: He has to support his wife and child, I wrote. How would he support Kaguya? She has never experienced any hardship, lacked food, or slept without a mattress. She's always pretty and clean. He wouldn't be able to take care of her. His wife wouldn't love her like I do.

Tuan Tan tapped the paper with his index finger and took the pen. His bold writing said: You have to choose. Can you imagine what will happen if the Indonesian militia arrest, imprison, or kill you? Who would take care of her?

Tears filled my eyes when I read his message. "I'll do anything as long as she does not suffer," I stammered.

"Do you trust me?" Tuan Tan slowly whispered the words. "Would you trust me to look after Kaguya?" he urged.

"What?" My mouth dropped open.

Tuan Tan grabbed the paper and I followed as he wrote: There's another temple at the junction of Selompretan Street and Coklat Street. It's the Hok An Kiong Temple— the oldest Chinese temple in Surabaya. You know it, don't you? While people come to this temple for worship and the Chinese send their children here for education, the Hok An Kiong Temple is used for worship and as a monastery. I know the caretaker. The temple also provides a shelter.

"I don't want Kaguya to be a Buddhist priest," I interrupted.

"No, that's not what I mean," he replied calmly, and continued to write.

You can temporarily entrust Kaguya to them. I'll talk to the caretaker. She'll be safe and won't lack for anything. She'll go to school and pray like the other children. She'll have a big family. You can leave her there and have peace of mind.

I was shocked.

Tuan Tan continued to explain on paper: After that I'll ask a Chinese ship captain, who happens to be related to me, to get you out of Indonesia. His merchant ship will pass Malaya and Singapore and dock in Peking. From there you take a train to Pusan in Korea, and then on to Japan. You'll leave Indonesia as Chinese, without anyone knowing your true nationality.

He looked up and cleared his throat before returning to his pen: Your journey at sea will be tiring and dangerous, and last for several months. It isn't possible to take your daughter, but it is the best way out of a difficult situation.

Later, when things are safe and back to normal, you can return for Kaguya's documents and take her to Japan. Isn't that better?

I could not speak. I was confused but I did not have another solution. I was attacked by many upsetting feelings I was unable to voice. Was there really no other way? Why then was it so difficult for me to make a decision? During my life, decisions were always made for me and when I chose to take charge of my future, I made a very big mistake that turned into a huge disaster. The experience frightened me so much I was reluctant to make another decision.

"Kaguya, would you like to stay with this grandpa?" I finally asked my daughter.

I was letting Kaguya determine our lives. It was actually a crazy, ridiculous, and foolish thing to do. How could a two-year-old make such an important choice? I was gambling with our lives.

Children have the purest form of intuition. I was not a coward—I simply could not do it and let Kaguya's intuition make the decision.

The little girl's round eyes blinked at me.

"Okasan?" she paused, and looked at me, puzzled.

"There's something Okasan has to do. I won't be long, darling. Mama will come back to pick you up soon."

Kaguya raised her head to meet the old eyes set on her. My little girl chuckled. She reached for Tuan Tan's pipe, took it from his hand, and, after examining it, put the pipe in the old man's mouth.

"Grandpa, Grandpa," she laughed.

"Look, she likes me. She trusts me." Tuan Tan held Kaguya's little hand, grinning.

"Trust me," he said slowly but firmly.

I had no other choice.

"I trust you." The words came from the agony in my heart.

*****

The ship's deck was crowded with smelly bodies and piles of goods. I was awake. My body trembled, and my teeth clattered. My stomach churned, and my throat was dry. My skin had darkened and my scalp was crusty. My eyelids were swollen from crying all the time and my eye sockets were sunken and sore. My body was mangled, but air still passed my nostrils. I was still breathing.

Circumstances strangled, but did not kill me.

Somehow, I remained alive.

What did Life actually want from me? I wanted to empty my faltering breath and let it ebb, swept by large waves. Let there be no more days and nights, no more clouds and rains, no more sea and heaven.

Life kept tossing me into His current. When I went with the flow, He threw me from one whirlpool into another.

When I decided to change direction and moor at a harbor, I crashed against rocks instead.

Life did not seem to be finished yet. He still insisted I measure the depth of the ocean and the breadth of the sky. But the ocean was so deep and the sky was so wide—I did not know where either would end.

A sharp pain dropped me into a storm of emotions.

Love? Hate? Regret? I was not sure.

I wept each time I was angry with myself. I regretted having made a decision I could not take back. Was I an irresponsible mother? I had left my little daughter in the middle of a war-torn country. I was selfish for thinking I could no longer shoulder the burden alone. Poor and unemployed, I had to cope with a man like Sujono while in a foreign country. I was not able to take it any longer.

Was I that heartless? I could not consider myself a decent mother. Anywhere on earth, a decent mother endured any amount of suffering for the sake of her child's happiness. She continued to fight. But what had I done? I ran from the problems and left my daughter to face the calamity by herself.

I ceaselessly cursed myself. I hated myself because all I could think of was how to leave the prison Sujono had built around my life. I wanted to set myself free from his shackles.

I lost the fight.

I gave up.

"Defeat" does not exist for a Japanese person.

But what had I done?

Defeat, despair, and weariness had made me selfish and caused me to leave Kaguya with an uncertain future. Even with the Allies defeating Japan and Indonesia becoming a new republic, even if the world came to an end, I should not have left my daughter.

I did not have anything to do with Japan although I am Japanese. Let the Emperor and the gods curse me for not supporting my country, but neither its defeat nor victory concerned me.

Indonesia, scrambling to establish a new republic, was none of my business, either. I did not care if the country was a colony or independent. Their president and its people could execute me in an open field when they discovered I was their enemy. I should have stayed with Kaguya regardless of any circumstance.

I should have taken her with me.

I shouldn't have left her.

I wept for my daughter. I remembered her fresh pink cheeks, black hair, round eyes with curly eyelashes, and her chatter that made me laugh.

What if she looked for me and cried? She had always been with me. How would she sleep? She had always slept by my side. I told her Japanese bedtime stories and sang lullabies, stroking her hair until she fell asleep. Who would put her to sleep now?

In my memory I went back to the evening I took Kaguya to the Hok An Kiong Temple and left her there.

Darkness had blanketed Surabaya's sky as I walked with Kaguya in my arms through the silence of the night. My chest ached and my heart pounded so hard I could hear its beat. Tuan Tan walked quietly beside me. We passed the deserted Kembang Jepun; all the shops were closed, no sign of people, and no lights. We continued to walk to the temple at the junction of Slompretan and Coklat Street.

The temple's gate and doors were locked when we arrived. It was very quiet. Tuan Tan knocked loudly. Soon, a teenage girl came running to open the gate and welcomed us inside.

The dim candlelight flickered from the wind when the door opened. There were huge candles as big as adults, little candles, and oil lamps. I also noticed the strong fragrance of incense sticks. I felt the eyes of the temple's gods upon us. Two tall statues of wide-eyed guards stood at the front door, and in the room behind was a big altar and a statue of the goddess of Thien Shang Sheng Mu. In the back room was the goddess Kwan Im Po Sat, who has one thousand hands. The Chinese worship her as the goddess of compassion, who hears the cries of people who are suffering. She is known as kindhearted and helps those in distress.

Would she hear my cries?

Would the holy goddess the Chinese worship, be kind and help me—Matsumi—a Japanese woman, despised by the Chinese?

Kaguya tightened her grip. She seemed to sense a new chapter in her journey; she was going to have her own encounters with Life. God only knew if she would flow, float, fly or drown. I knew she was afraid because I had the same fear.

I sat on a long red bench at the left side of the temple and faced Kwan Im Po's shrine. Near the bench stood a building used as a place of residence like a dormitory for the temple's caretaker and her foster children. All of the children seemed to be girls. I heard from Tuan Tan that the female caretaker of the temple was not married and stayed at the shrine to look after it and the girls. They called her Mama Nio.

We didn't wait long before a woman in her fifties met us with a big, friendly smile. She did not seem to be disturbed by our sudden visit. Like Tuan Tan, she gave me a cup of tea to warm me.

Apparently Mama Nio knew Tuan Tan. They nodded at each other and she spoke to him in Chinese. Now and then, she nodded her head while turning to Kaguya and me.

After they finished talking Tuan Tan walked toward me and patted my shoulder. Smiling, he said, "Don't worry. I have explained everything and she is willing to take Kaguya."

The Chinese woman gave me another friendly smile. The wrinkles at the corners of her eyes emanated peace and sincerity. We had made a good decision to go to the temple.

"Call me Mama Nio, just like the other girls," she introduced herself.

I set Kaguya on the floor. It was time for us to part. I could not stay longer. I had to rush, although I wished time would stop. I did not want to leave Kaguya and again I felt that Life was unfair. He never gave me a chance to choose and always forced me to follow what He had planned for me. Was I a coward for always making Life a scapegoat?

I kissed Kaguya's pink cheeks and looked at her face. Soon I would be thousands of miles away from her. I wanted to paint her face on the wall of my heart so I could see her all the time, like when she was close to me.

I did not have any explanation for a two-year-old girl, and it was not necessary. I did not need to explain because there was no choice; our circumstance was very painful.

"Okasan is leaving soon. You be a good girl and stay here with this grandma. Mama will come back for you. Do you understand, Kaguya?" My voice trembled; the pain was overwhelming.

Although I wanted to say so much, those were the only words I could stammer. Could words make her understand? What use were words when they only deepened the pain?

"Here's Grandpa and here's Grandma," my little girl murmured. She clearly had not understood me.

Mama Nio reached for Kaguya's hand and held it with motherly tenderness. She seemed to understand our anxiety and wanted to hold us in her warmth. "Don't worry. Try to feel at ease. I'll take care of Kaguya," Mama Nio assured me.

I asked her for a piece of paper and wrote KAGUYA in kanji. I handed the paper to my little girl, tears flowing down my face.

"Here is your name. Keep it. You're Japanese. You have to return to Japan," I sobbed.

My little girl looked at the paper. She was confused but nodded and smiled. She might have thought it was something to play with, but one day when she had grown up, she would know it was a testament of her life's journey.

"*Haik, haik*, yes." she said repeatedly, her small head swaying.

I knew she did not understand.

I did not want to spend more time in the temple, because the Chinese ship set sail before sunrise and I could not afford to miss the opportunity. Besides, I was afraid I would change my mind if I stayed longer. I was scared I would not leave Kaguya, and create an even more difficult problem.

"Uncle Tan and Auntie Nio, I entrust Kaguya to you. I trust you. *Arigato gozaimasu, arigato gozaimasu,*" I addressed the two elderly Chinese according to their custom and thanked them by bowing as deep as I could.

I left Kaguya in their care and gathered my things. I didn't have much, just clothes from the Boen Bio Temple.

Then, pushed by a force outside myself, I walked to the shrine of Kwan Im Po, the goddess with one thousand hands. The flames of the oil lamps and candles flickered, and the aroma of the incense blended with the fragrance of flowers, entered my nostrils with the air I breathed. I bowed deeply in front of the shrine and clasped my hands to worship the goddess. I could not hold my tears.

As a teenager, I often prayed at the shrine in Gion, always asking to become a geisha, a beautiful princess. But then I prayed for my dream without shedding any tears.

My wish came true: I did become the most popular geisha, but then I left, and the dream blew away like a gust of wind.

Now I came with all my shortcomings and again bowed deeply in prayer. Did she listen to me?

I did not care Kwan Im Po was Chinese.

I did not care I was on the island of Java.

I did not care whether she listened to me or not.

All that is holy comes from the conscience. Because of the war, there was much anger, vengeance, hate, and pain that made wounds too deep to heal. Those sins spread everywhere. Blood spewed from the sky and ashes erupted from the earth. I prayed to submit everything at her shrine, because I was weak—I did not have anything.

I belonged to Kwan Im Po.

I clasped my hands, holding the million pains that filled my heart. I did not ask to become a princess anymore. Instead, I had brought one—Kaguya—and I asked the goddess to look after her.

I heard the elderly man and woman behind me heave a long sigh.

"Poor woman. I hope Kwan Im Po will protect her," Mama Nio whispered.

I prayed for a long time. I did not care if the goddess of compassion understood the prayer I delivered in Japanese. All of the most holy have the sensitivity to understand pains and prayers expressed in different languages.

When I finally stepped out of the temple's gate, I hardened my heart not to look back. I vaguely heard Kaguya running after me and calling, "Okasan."

Sujono had made me abandon my daughter.

I really hated him.

Part 4: Sujono

Surabaya 1943–1945

I am a bastard.

After the Allies dropped atom bombs on Hiroshima and Nagasaki, news of Japan's defeat spread across the country by radio, newspapers, and announcements posted in the streets. Indonesian revolutionaries took immediate action. They proclaimed the country's independence, started forming a new government, took control of important institutions, and disarmed the Japanese soldiers. Japanese citizens were required to register and interned at the Kalisosok Prison while waiting to be returned to their country by ship. What would happen next was uncertain because of the change of power.

That morning I was very anxious when I did not find Matsumi at her house. The yard was quiet. I could find no one, not even Karmi, Matsumi's maid.

I was worried. Matsumi never left the house without me. Although she tried to be Chinese, she felt awkward among the Chinese women who lived in the neighborhood. That's why she never went to the market. Karmi shopped for her. I always accompanied Matsumi when she went for a walk. Otherwise she just stayed home, playing with Kaguya, making orisurus near the window, and letting the sunshine stroke her ivory skin. Sometimes I was jealous of the sun that could enjoy her skin all the time.

I met Matsumi as the star of a club in Kembang Jepun. She often bought cloth from the shop owned by Babah Oen, the Chinese merchant I worked for. Babah Oen sent me to the club to deliver the orders. That gave me the chance to see her more often.

"Aiya, it's good to be a little bit busier. Business is very difficult with the war. The shop is quiet. Even to eat is hard now, let alone buy clothes. Luckily there are geishas who must always wear new dresses," Babah Oen said, when he sent me on a delivery. The rise and fall of his Chinese pronunciation changed r's into l's.

I did not mind making deliveries to Hanada-san's club. It was a task I looked forward to because it gave me the opportunity to see its most famous, charming woman.

Her name was Tjoa Kim Hwa and she was referred to as Golden Flower. At first I thought she was Chinese like most of the women in the club. Only a few of them were Javanese. However, later it turned out that she was Japanese—her real name was Matsumi.

Rumors said she was once the most popular geisha in her country. This did not surprise me. Matsumi was a gorgeous woman and very seductive. She made men's heart race with her smile. Her sideways glances left them breathless as they tried to control their passion. Their desire to make love to her was certain.

Matsumi had a fair and luminous oval face, with eyes not as narrow as those of many Japanese women. Her mouth was small, genuinely small, not shaped with lip rouge to look little. She had small straight teeth. I often peeked into her kimono's sleeves and saw the ivory skin of her arms when she took the fabric order from me. She walked with fairly quick small steps and sometimes I saw the long deep curve above her heels under her kimono.

The Javanese said that a woman with such a curve gave extraordinary pleasure in bed, and Matsumi had such a heel. Another Javanese belief was that a woman's skin should not be too fair because it would be dull, or too dark because it would be unattractive. Matsumi's skin was ivory. Men like women with full lips that close into an attractively shaped mouth. Matsumi's lips were perfectly shaped, and enticed men.

People call me a bastard, a bastard who likes "beautiful things." I think that is normal. God gave man eyes to see beauty, and created the senses to enjoy pleasure. It is normal for a man to desire beauty and pleasure, and Matsumi had both.

I can't deny I fell in love with her. I was in love with how she looked as well as the inner beauty she exuded. It was not an overstatement to say Matsumi was the perfect woman: she had a pretty face, a gracefully shaped body, and a fragrant scent. She was gentle, intelligent, and had a sense of art. She sang like a lark, cleverly arranged words into poetry, played the shamisen with her slim fingers dancing gracefully over the strings, and was skillful at serving people. She was very good at making men happy, spoiling them, and making them feel like a king in her presence.

I often watched her accompany guests at the club. I also saw her treat a guest to the bathing ritual in the ofuro at the back of the club, until they went to one of the rooms and disappeared behind its sliding door. I heard them talk for a while until their voices softened to whispers that turned into grunts, sighs, and finally an uncontrollable long whine.

The more I saw Matsumi the more I wanted to be with her. When I tried to look at her secretly, she caught me immediately and her melancholic eyes met with mine, arousing me.

Once I accidentally saw her soaking in the ofuro. I had to drop off her fabric order. That afternoon the club was still quiet; no one was at the front and I went straight to the back to make the delivery.

There I saw a naked body in the ofuro. She had a smooth ivory neck, shoulders, and back, so smooth a mosquito might slip when it landed. I held my breath and enjoyed the beautiful sight before me. She stood and left the tub, while I enjoyed another view of her heavenly perfect body: full, round, young breasts with a pink small nipple, small waist, flat stomach, curvy hips, and long legs. I did not allow my eyes to blink. I tried hard to control myself so I would not grab her naked body and pull her into one of the rooms.

Matsumi noticed me and was shocked. She stared at me, then scrambled for her kimono, threw it around her body, and ran soaking wet to her room.

Since then I was determined to sleep with her, like her other rich guests. I asked how much it cost to purchase her service. It turned out to be very expensive; I would have to fast for two years to save up enough. Also, she did not entertain just any guest, only high-ranking military officers and wealthy men.

In my desperation, one day, I stole money from Babah Oen's shop. They found out and I was fired, but I did not care. I could get a job as a coolie anywhere.

Matsumi was surprised. She did not expect I was the guest waiting in her room, and turned awkward. I knew she was not used to serving a poor man like me. She did not know how to carry herself. She knew what to do with Shosho Kobayashi and other wealthy guests, how to make them happy and lead them to perfect satisfaction. She served those guests with the attributes that came with being the most desired geisha, but now she stood rigid and looked confused. With my desire raging, I took her into my arms. I held her tight before undressing her. After exploring her entire body with all my senses and savoring every inch, I finally went inside her.

At first her smooth, cool body tensed, but she soon started to warm. Her sweet breath blew on my ear, and soft sighs and whimpers passed her lips while her wriggling body eagerly met my movements. Watching her sigh with her eyes closed peaked my desire. Our bodies tensed for a moment before we turned limp in each other's arms. I ended our game of passion with a long deep kiss.

I was completely satisfied.

*****

After that time, Matsumi and I became closer. I was really in love with her, not only physically, but also emotionally. I pulled her into the arms of my desire and breathed wild passion with her. I made our love flourish. I was mad about her and loved her to death. Seeing her serve her guests made me jealous and resentful. The scent of other men on her body made me angry and the thought of their sweat on her skin tortured me. I did not want other men to sleep with her. I wanted her to be my wife. I wanted her to be mine alone.

With Matsumi, I was a man in love, drunk on her beauty and charms. I may have been shameless as I was only a coolie while she was the most popular geisha. Honestly, I often felt like an owl yearning for the moon. I watched and enjoyed her from a distance with all my heart, and carried her into my dreams.

Is falling in love only for the rich? A coolie like me also has the right to fall in love. Was it because I was poor that I could not have the Golden Flower? Was I wrong to fall in love when I already had a wife and child? I was dissatisfied with my life. My burning desire for Matsumi gave me courage to pursue her. I was so in love. I did not want to share her with other men.

My desire to have Matsumi entirely mine made me lose sight of everything else. I wanted to make her pregnant. I wanted to have a daughter as lovely as her, a child from her womb. I repeatedly told Matsumi my dream until she finally wanted the same thing. A woman's destiny is to get pregnant and give birth. I talked her into changing her mind from never wanting a child to desiring one.

I wanted more than a child from Matsumi. I wanted her and her child. By having a child, she would be absolutely mine. Giving birth would change her beautiful body so she would no longer be able to work as a geisha. She would sleep and wake up beside me. How wonderful the days would be if my beloved Matsumi was the first thing I saw when I opened my eyes.

I may have been married and already had a child, but I did not care. My feelings toward Matsumi were incomparable to those I had toward my wife, Sulis.

Finally Matsumi became pregnant.

How happy I was when she told me that she was heavy with child. I kissed every part of her face until she gasped and her cheeks turned red. I was over the moon. Matsumi was mine alone.

Imagine my pride: I, Sujono, only a coolie, was the husband of Matsumi, the most desired woman in Kembang

Jepun. Out of the many rich men who were crazy about her, she had chosen me.

I felt very different from the time Sulis told me about her pregnancy. Then I did not feel proud, glad, or happy. Instead I was angry because she had used me, forcing me to marry her because she claimed to be having my child.

Sulis and I met shortly before we were married. She was a jamu peddler; many coolies along Gula Street often bought her potions.

Sulis was not pretty. Her skin was dark, her eyes big and defiant, and her lips thick. She also had big breasts and coarse black hair. But she was a flirt. She pouted when someone teased her and also liked to giggle. Maybe she did that to attract many customers.

I liked teasing her. I took advantage of her and owed her for jamu—a debt I never paid. I also liked touching her because she gave me the opportunity. She wore a low-cut kebaya, sometimes leaving one button undone so men could see her black bra. She also wore her kain high as if she wanted to show off her legs as she walked. She sat without keeping her knees together and tended to draw her legs apart. Her body language was vulgar and her eyes invited men to tease, touch, kiss, and sleep with her.

I was forced to marry her because she was pregnant.

It was truly an accident, and she trapped me. A bastard like me had slept with many women. I knew how to do it without causing pregnancy, but I was very drunk when I did it with Sulis and could not recall what I had done. All the coolies working along Coklat Street knew she was

Mas Wandi's secret mistress. I did not have the slightest intention of being serious with her and had even prepared for marriage with another girl. I doubt that Joko is my son and I don't have any affection for him.

Matsumi was different.

Although many men slept with her, I loved her. I was determined to make her fall in love with me, and she did. I experienced an incredible passion when sleeping with her. It was very different from sleeping with Sulis, which I often did only out of duty. It was a bland and false pleasure, where with Matsumi, the passion was tumultuous. Our squirms and moans raced to the point of what she called deep yonaki.

The child in Matsumi's womb was mine. I was an experienced man who could tell the difference between soulful lovemaking and the mere union between two sexual organs.

I asked Matsumi to leave Hanada-san's club because I did not want to share her with other men. She obeyed me and left the club on Kembang Jepun, and gave birth to Kaguya for me.

She bought a house near Kapasan Street, owned by a Chinese and very large compared to my tiny room. It was even too big for Matsumi, Kaguya, and the maid. The windows and doors were always wide open. Sunlight entered the house freely and the air blew in and out through the shutters. The ceilings were high so the inside was cool. The yard was spacious, too.

"I used most of my savings to buy this house. We'll have many children so we need one that is big enough," she said.

She lived there with Kaguya and a maid to help with their daily needs. Every morning I went to the house and enjoyed a life full of honey. The difficulties that bound me to Sulis disappeared magically. I did not have any trouble when staying with Matsumi. She was as sweet as candy and took care of me from head to toe. She made me a real man. She not only satisfied me on the futon but also quenched my thirst for life.

Matsumi was a good woman. My head did not ache from thinking about money for cigarettes, rice, side dishes, or groceries. She even gave me money to meet Sulis's kitchen needs. I no longer needed to work myself into a sweat and burn my skin under the sun, lifting rolls of textiles for Babah Oen. All I needed to do was make love.

Making love. Wonderful, wasn't it? Very different from the life Sulis gave me.

Matsumi knew how difficult it was to live in a war-torn country. She knew I was poor, and many times unable to buy rice. So she bought things for Sulis, not only rice, but also eggs, vegetables, and fish. She knew I did not have a good education so I could not work in an office. She knew I was not an office worker, only a laborer doing rough work.

She understood I wanted to join the resistance movement. I often imagined myself in a military uniform carrying a rifle over my shoulder. I would stand boldly in a line with other soldiers, defending my motherland and claiming independence. That was what many of us dreamed of right then. With independence, we would be a dignified nation, not an oppressed people who worked as forced laborers under the Dutch and Japanese. We would have the right over our own country.

Slowly, military rank and medals would line up on my shoulders and arms. I would be like Sudirman. Wouldn't that be something to be proud of rather than thickening my shoulders and arms from carrying Babah Oen's textile rolls? With the line of medals I would have dignity, not only be a coolie who made Chinese people richer by working for them cheaply. Later, I would tell my children and grandchildren I was one of those who helped found this country.

Sulis never appreciated my dreams. She was more concerned with her own life. Added to it were a child's whimpers that made our tiny room even smaller. I did not feel at home with her.

The woman used Joko to hold me back. She did not allow me to join the resistance although many young men joined Defenders of the Homeland, where the Japanese gave military training to Javanese people. Sulis's reason was simple—she did not want to be a widow while still young and with a small child. With the birth of Joko, she forced me to take any kind of work. She did not care if I had to be a Japanese romusha, as long as I fed the open mouths in our small room.

She was right when she said it was my responsibility, but she never appreciated my passion for nationalism. She did not care if I had no dignity as long as cooking smoke rose from her kitchen.

I don't know who was right or wrong, but I was disappointed at being bound by the chains of marriage and trapped by the child. The marriage, wife, and child hampered my steps—I could not walk freely.

Sulis said she also felt trapped in our marriage and imprisoned by poverty. She always complained that I was not responsible. She regretted getting married to me.

Responsible?

Hadn't I been responsible by marrying her? Hadn't I been responsible by being willing to take any job, whatever it was, to keep food in our mouths? I worked as a coolie at a very meager wage, just enough to buy rice and cigarettes. I buried my dream to fight for my homeland for her.

What kind of responsibility did she want?

Sulis was relentless. She always demanded more, beyond what I could afford.

"I'm sick of living like a beggar, sick of being poor," she said when the money I gave her was only enough for the day.

I did not answer. I just shrugged my shoulders; the taste of my cigarette was more pleasant than listening to her clamor. I did not want another long tiring fight with her. It was enough to lift textile rolls, each the size of a grown man, all day long at Babah Oen's shop. What I needed at home was rest, not grumbles about poverty.

Poverty was like a ghost: No one wanted to approach it, summon it with a smile, or welcome it when it arrived. It comes although we never want it to. It has no form so we cannot avoid it. Poverty attaches itself to our lives by adding problem after problem.

"Mas, you're an utterly irresponsible man. You never take care of me and Joko."

"Don't you have enough to eat? Is Joko starving?" I argued and started to feel upset.

"I'm sick of eating rice with only sweet soy sauce. Even our neighbors have tofu and tempeh," Sulis started with her demand for things.

"You should be grateful we still have rice, even if it is with nothing but soy sauce. Many people out there only eat once a day. They have to fast because they don't have money for rice."

"Why compare us with people who are worse off than us? It will never get us a better life," she shot back, her eyes bulging.

I hated seeing her eyes when she was angry. Not only because they looked huge—nearly as big as ping pong balls—but also because their veins turn red. I did not like looking at her fearless gaze, challenging and attacking me. It is not proper for a woman to glare at any man, let alone her husband, with her hands riding on her hips. Very disrespectful.

"Everyone would have a better life if our country was free, if it worked to feed its own people, and foreign nations did not wring the wealth out of us. Colonialists. Fuck," I started cursing.

"When will we be free?" Sulis sneered. "That means we'll stay poor forever," she railed while twisting her thick lips from side to side.

"Indonesia could be independent if all the people have the spirit to fight, and not only think about their own stomach like you," I accused her.

"What?" Again she widened her eyes. "Is it wrong to be concerned about my own stomach? How can I care about other people when I'm starving?"

Ugh. I was sick to death of hearing the words that came out of her mouth. I loathed seeing how she held her body, her face, and her eyes. Was she the woman I married? She was a monster that kept saying "responsible" to harass me. She was rude, greedy, ambitious, and not a nationalist. She was also clever at taking advantage of our situation to burden me with "the responsibility for our child." Arggh.

I was furious when she decided to sell jamu again. She said she needed to make ends meet; it was only an excuse to avoid what was supposed to be her responsibility. Not only men have responsibilities. Women do, too.

Take care of the house, child, and me—Sulis never did any of this. She neglected our home; it was filthy and full with dirty clothes; mice scurried around the kitchen. The sleeping mats were carelessly rolled up and left lying around. She let Joko play on the muddy soil naked and with snot running down his nose. Meanwhile she would sit around with the women from neighboring rooms. While searching each other's head for lice, they would giggle over stories about their man's performance. When I came home, all she offered was drinking water and dried white rice with sweet soy sauce a cat might have sniffed.

Sulis did not treat me like a husband.

She did not respect me.

She wanted to sell jamu because she missed her flirting. She wanted men to tease her and her to tease them. I admit to giving her very little money. It was barely enough to feed the family and she used this as a reasonable excuse.

I did not mind if she sold jamu. It would free me from the pressure of not being able to meet the family needs. But I knew selling herbal potions was to annoy and shame me. The whole kampung would know that she had to work to feed the family. They would sneer at me. Also, she passed her responsibility for taking care of the child, who was still little, to me.

Sulis could not make me feel jealous but she tortured me about responsibility. I, too, was entitled to demand responsibility from her. She forced me to work, besieged me with her grumbles, was never content with the money I gave her, and never understood how much I loved this country.

She imprisoned me.

With all my hatred, I locked her in our tiny room to meet my demands. I used her as a target for my disappointment.

Was our marriage a hell? I did not care. Life with her already felt like a thorn in my flesh. Wasn't that worse than hell?

I finally destroyed her bottles so that she could not peddle jamu. She was mad, bulged her eyes and put her hands on her hips in front of me. I felt sick hearing the demands spill out of her wide mouth while watching her vulgar display. I punched one of her bulging eyes; a bruise instantly appeared. I hit her babbling mouth; fresh blood flowed down from the cut at the corner of her lips. I raped her short and dark body. I bit her huge nipples and the blackened skin surrounding them. I lifted her legs, pressed them against her chest, and turned her body over like a sate stick on a bed of coals. I had sex with her for hours without any passion.

There was no lust or pleasure. I wanted to teach her a lesson for flirting. I wanted her to feel pain and learn not to bulge her eyes, put her hands on the hips, and curse in front of me.

We were like a pair of wrestlers grappling and slamming each other on the floor. The more she fought back, the rougher I became.

Strangely, she seemed to enjoy it. She reached orgasm again and again.

I did not want to finish the play by squirting inside her. This was not making love. It did not give me pleasure. It was not delightful. I did not have the desire to enjoy sex with her.

Matsumi was very different.

Her house was always tidy and clean. The futon smelled fresh, the food was hot and appetizing, and Kaguya always looked pretty and smelled nice.

While she had a maid to help take care of the house, Matsumi always served me herself. She bathed me, made me smell good, and served my food decently. She also hugged me affectionately and kissed me with passion.

I never felt I was a coolie with Matsumi. She made me feel worthy, a perfect man with dignity. She was so elegant with her beauty and charming with her softness. Her smiles, laughter, and the way she spoke were gentle and graceful. She made love with tenderness and soulfulness. Her naked body was beautiful, soft, smooth and warm. She excited me just by looking at her, without touching. I always ended our lovemaking with a long, fulfilled yonaki.

Was it only lust?

No.

I was infatuated, in love and lovesick.

I always looked at her, touched, caressed, kissed, and slept with her with overflowing love. I made love with great yearning and all my burning passion.

Matsumi was different from Sulis.

*****

I looked for Matsumi in every corner of her house. I checked every room but I did not find her. The kitchen was also empty. The yard was abandoned and I did not even catch a glimpse of her shadow, only the evaporating scent of her body. I began to worry and panic. The fear of losing her started to grip me. My gut feeling told me that something had happened.

Since Matsumi had given birth to Kaguya, she repeatedly told me she wanted to work again at Hanada-san's club in Kembang Jepun.

"I'm running out of savings. We don't have any more money and need a lot to live on. I must go to work again."

"I don't like you working there. I don't like you sleeping with so many men."

"No, I won't sleep with the guests. I'll just play the shamisen and sing, sit and talk with the guests, and serve sake."

"What if they ask you to entertain them in the back room?"

"I'll refuse."

"I don't believe it. I know that kind of life too well," I laughed without knowing why I was laughing.

"So?" she asked.

I could not give her an answer.

I was a selfish man. I loved Matsumi. I could not let her work at the club, but I was also unable to fulfill her needs. My wages were not even enough to feed Sulis and Joko. The truth was that since I knew Matsumi, she spent more money on them than I did. Sometimes I felt useless. My own earnings were not enough to meet my household's basic needs, let alone take care of Matsumi and Kaguya. We used Matsumi's savings for everyone.

Sulis once asked me where the money came from, as we never had enough before. I did not like her asking about it. That I only could feed my family with Matsumi's help already made me feel inferior. She didn't have to needle me about where the money came from.

Besides, I was tired of Sulis complaining about our poverty. I gagged her mouth with the money from Matsumi to lighten my burden. At least I slept peacefully at night without having to think about how we would eat the next day.

Matsumi also had to make her ends meet. I was sorry I could not give her a better life. Instead, I dragged her into suffering. She was now part of my destitution and poverty.

She always said, "Stay with me. You love me, don't you? I want you by my side. There are many problems but if we face them together, it will not be that hard. If you stay with me we could open a small shop. You can run it. We would not be short of money."

That was what I wanted, too. So far I only went to Matsumi's house early in the morning and went back to Sulis's tiny room at night. I was sick of my harsh life. I did not want to return to poverty.

But Sulis made trouble. She started inquiring about Matsumi.

"Who is Matsumi? You talked in your sleep, Mas. She's a whore in Kembang Jepun, isn't she? No wonder you've got a lot of money now. You've become a Nippon whore's kept husband." Sulis spoke with her thick lips twisting from side to side. Her big eyes glared.

I might have talked in my sleep and mentioned Matsumi. Unless I was drunk, she was always in my mind. When I returned to the room, only my body went home; my mind and soul stayed with Matsumi. I was always thinking of her.

I longed for her. I wanted the sun to rise quickly so I could go back to her arms.

"Don't think you can be a kept husband, Mas. The whole kampung is talking about you."

What Sulis said hurt my dignity.

"People know Nippon whores have a lot of money because they serve many guests. You should ask her to buy you a house. I'm sick of living in this tiny room. No use if you don't get anything," Sulis demanded.

Was I that low in her eyes? I felt she was selling me to meet our living needs. Cunningly she had used her pregnancy to force me into marriage. Now she tried using me to free herself from the bondage of poverty.

That woman was really wicked.

I stared at her furiously, but all I found in her glaring eyes was satisfaction. She was happy when she could insult me and hurt my pride.

I no longer saw a woman in front of me; she was a poisonous scorpion. She could bite and squirt her venom whenever she wanted.

"Why? What did I say wrong?" she sneered.

I clenched my teeth to hold off my anger.

"When I was a peddler, you said I slept with Nippon soldiers to sell more jamu. Now it turns out you are serving a Nippon whore. Why? Every service has its reward, right?"

Gosh.

Her tongue was fiery. Every word that came out of her mouth hurt my dignity. She made me hate her even more, and unable to hold my fist from punching her face.

Matsumi and Sulis were as different as heaven and earth. They were like bright morning and gloomy night, a beautiful angel and poisonous evil. Was it wrong if I felt tortured living with Sulis?

When she started grumbling about the many things we needed, the tone of her voice started to rise. She screamed hysterically until the neighbors along the alley looked at us. She did not care. She glared at me while pointing her finger to the door.

"Get out of here. Run away with your Nippon whore. I'll get the drunks at the end of the alley to rape her." She roared as if she was making an announcement to the whole kampung. She intentionally did that to shame me. It was also her way to let go of her anger with me, and she would continue unless I stopped her.

I punched her evil mouth and blood flowed from the corner of her cut lips. Instead of turning quiet, she became fierce as a wounded lioness. She spat blood-mixed saliva on the floor. It seemed she was unable to feel pain or fear.

"Argh. Was I wrong? You say you love this country. Aren't you very proud of your people? Indonesians have suffered enough being occupied by the Nippon. They have harassed and raped many Indonesian women and made them pregnant. That is an insult, isn't it? Where is your nationalism? Now it's our turn to rape the Nippon whore. Why do you defend her instead?" Her words shot from her mouth like bullets out of a rifle.

"I want to know if you could marry that Nippon. I dare you. Go ahead and leave Joko and me for that bitch. I know where she lives. I'll get the kampung people to strip her naked on the street.

"Once a whore always a whore. Slut! Bitch! Disgusting!" Shuddering, she spat more saliva mixed with blood on the floor.

Sulis held me back. She became more demanding, threatened to hurt Matsumi, and used my responsibility to Joko as a shield. I was unable to move forward or backward—she clenched me like an octopus with many tentacles. She made every day difficult.

Most Indonesians hated the Japanese people, including Matsumi. Even worse, she was a courtesan. She always cautioned me not to let anyone know she was Japanese. She told people she was Chinese.

I could not do anything but protect her from the possibility of being assaulted by people from the kampung.

Kampung people were different from soldiers. Soldiers would capture a Japanese to get information, detain, or maybe kill them. But if people from the kampung caught Matsumi, they would insult, shame, and degrade her, and worse if Sulis told them she had seduced her husband. On top of throwing stones at her house and looting it, they would strip her naked, rape, and even parade her.

I did not want to imagine what might happen to Matsumi. And since I would not let anything happen to her, I was crippled.

Matsumi slowly distanced herself from me. She became quiet. I often saw her sit silently watching the sunset through the window. Sometimes she did not listen when I talked to her. She stared blankly at Kaguya, her hands folding the origami paper into a crane and putting it on the table after she finished.

I suspected that Matsumi's love for me was getting weaker. She still served me—from food to making love—like before, but my heart told me she was becoming distant. Her body was close to me but her heart and thoughts wandered somewhere else. The suspicion tortured me. I did not feel her heart was with me and I was scared of losing her.

"I won't let you leave me," I told her.

Matsumi now was not the Matsumi who was warm on the futon. She did not close her eyes with her lips half opened while making love. Instead, she gave me a cold cynical look.

"I want to be like the bird coming from Amaterasu Omikami, the sun goddess, and returning to her again. I miss Kyoto and Gion," she whispered softly, as if talking to herself in her own world.

I embraced her, kissing her again and again.

"No. Your place is right here, by my side. You are in Indonesia and have become an Indonesian. I won't let you leave me," I tried to persuade her.

She was cold.

She did not feel pleasure or give pleasure.

Instead, her cold, sharp stare was filled with hatred. It made me quiver. She only showed hurt and hate when our eyes met.

"You have Kaguya. You can't leave her," I said, out of my fear of losing her.

I used Kaguya often to shake off her sharp, stabbing look. The mention of Kaguya softened her eyes. Oh, they did not really soften, but turned away to look at the sun.

I learned to be like Sulis and slyly imitating how she used Joko to chain me, I used Kaguya to stop Matsumi from leaving.

Was I selfish? Yes. My love for her made me so selfish.

She smiled coldly. "I'm Japanese so I must return to Japan," she said, heaving a long sigh.

That was the only thing she said.

I knew she suffered from living with me. She wanted to free herself from the bonds of love I had fastened to her feet. She was not happy.

But again, my extraordinary love for her had made me selfish. I did not want to let her go and did not care if she was happy with me or not. What I knew was I was happy having Matsumi.

Was it wrong to have such a one-sided love? Did I clap with only one hand? I could not hear any sound like when using two hands. My palm only hit the air.

It was worse after the Japanese lost the war against the Allies. Indonesian youth took the opportunity to proclaim our independence and founded the republic. As I heard from a neighbor's radio, Soekarno and Hatta would arrange for transfer of power from the Japanese.

The last news I heard was that all Japanese in Indonesia would be registered and returned to their country. Many Japanese soldiers committed seppuku when they heard about the defeat. Many died. Our soldiers disarmed the

Japanese soldiers who were still alive and immediately closed and sealed the clubs along Kembang Jepun. The women at the kurabus, who the Japanese soldiers punished with their lust, had saved their own lives. They freed themselves from hell and went anywhere they thought was safe and away from the soldiers.

I was very worried that Matsumi would return to Japan, but I shook off the thought; I believed she would not leave Kaguya. I always used the child as hostage so Matsumi would not leave me. She would not be able to take Kaguya to Japan without complete documents from the Japanese government.

But today the house was dead quiet. Where was Matsumi?

I spotted a piece of paper under the piles of orisuru on the table. Trembling, I took it and read Matsumi's handwriting in very simple Indonesian, "Matsumi comes from Amaterasu Omikami. Matsumi returns to it."

My body felt like mush. I sat down and my eyes were teary. I felt I had lost all of my soul—as if the air flowing in and out of my nostrils was gone.

Matsumi had left me.

I felt like I was dead. She had taken all of my heart, and I did not know where to look for her. She was the only woman who had made me fall in love and also deeply hurt me. The pain was so sharp it made me tremble.

I wanted to search for her, drag her away, and take her home. Matsumi mustn't return to Japan.

Would she have joined the Japanese prisoners at Kalisosok? I wanted to run there, go through the prison's thick wall, and look for her. But there were thousands of Japanese. How could I find her? Would she even be there? I was only Sujono, a coolie, an ordinary person, a commoner—I could not enter the prison to look for someone who used to be the most desirable woman in Kembang Jepun. I was not a man with the authority to inspect all the Japanese in the prison.

A glimpse of my little girl passed in my mind.

Kaguya. Where is she? Matsumi couldn't take her to Japan. Had she left her behind? Impossible, my heart said. So where are they? They couldn't be far. I must find them.

*****

The mood of Surabaya was uneasy.

The Japanese defeat had crippled the city. No one would go out on the street unless they were forced. Only soldiers walked the streets, Allies and Indonesians, and Japanese soldiers who had been arrested or surrendered. The marching steps of the soldiers made the streets dusty. People were afraid of getting searched while others chose to follow the news from the radio.

I did neither.

I spent days walking along the streets of Kembang Jepun, looking for Matsumi and Kaguya. I did not really know where I should go to find them. First I went to Hanada-san's club, but it was already closed and sealed. They had taken the owner to jail.

Without fear, I walked back and forth in front of the former Japanese military headquarters. I tried to peek inside, thinking Matsumi might have gone there. I did not see a glimpse of her. The building was cold, dark, gloomy, and seemed haunted. Too many people had died there, and turned into ghosts that roamed the building. People still heard screams and cries coming from inside, and shadows of headless bodies were seen moving back and forth in the dark. It was an evil building.

Matsumi could not have taken Kaguya there. I also asked her neighbors where they might have gone, but all I got were headshakes and doors shut in my face. Karmi, her maid, had gone God knows where. I felt as if I was searching for a needle in a haystack.

Everyone waited for the new government's next step. What would Soekarno and Hatta do for the new republic? Meanwhile, what would I do with my life?

I was really desperate. I locked Matsumi's house.

When despair and yearning tortured me, I would go to the house and sit inside. Nothing had changed. Through the large open windows the sun light still came in to warm the rooms. There were paper cranes piled on a table, the pretty little cups Matsumi used for the tea ceremony, a futon on the tatami, and several nicely folded kimonos. The fragrance of her powder had not left the house, although the dust piled up and spiders built their webs. The breeze coming into the house felt humid because the house was empty.

Meanwhile in the tiny room I shared with Sulis, she made noises again about money: shouting, screaming, scowling, harassing, smashing a plate, and banging the door.

"Where's the money, Mas? There's nothing to eat for tomorrow."

"I've got none. Let's just fast."

"Fast?" She went wide-eyed.

I hated those eyes.

"Joko can't fast," she screamed.

"What can I do? The Chinese shops have closed. No one will give me a job. As you can see, everyone is staying at home."

She shrugged her shoulders.

"Well, it depends on how you do it, Mas."

"How? You tell me."

Sulis grumbled. "Do you have to work at a Chinese shop? You can work at the harbor, push a pedicab, or peddle ice, anything, as long as we don't starve."

I was quiet.

Her complaints were hurtful.

"You're the kept husband of a Nippon whore who has a lot of money. But it's useless if you can't even buy rice."

My ears began to burn.

"Have you gone poor again? Have they arrested her and sent her home? Poor woman. Sorry." Her thick lips twisted in every direction.

I started to be angry but tried to keep calm.

I chose to leave. I wanted to look for Matsumi and Kaguya. That was more useful than listening to her poisonous words.

"Where are you going?" she asked.

"You told me to do something," I answered indifferently. To find Matsumi and Kaguya, my heart said.

I turned a deaf ear to the loud bang of the door behind me. I roamed the streets afraid and anxious. On Kapasan Street lined with cotton trees, the fenced houses of the rich Chinese were tightly shut, along with the Boen Bio Temple. I walked tirelessly. My sweat made my shirt wet.

Kembang Jepun was quiet and Babah Oen's shop on Coklat Street was closed. Across from the Hok An Kiong Temple was a small coffee stand.

The sun shone above my head. Surabaya kept getting hotter.

I reached into my pant's pocket for my remaining several cent coins, enough for a cup of coffee to wet my throat and a cigarette to get rid of the tart-bitter taste in my mouth.

I sat hunched over my coffee. My thoughts drifted with the plumes of smoke from my cigarette. Only two other people—pedicab drivers—were having coffee. I looked at the cup in front of me. It was very black, dark as the way ahead as I did not know where to find Matsumi and Kaguya.

"Bad for business if it stays this quiet," the old woman who owned the stand mumbled.

"Yes. No one is leaving the house. I hardly had any passengers either," complained one of the pedicab drivers.

"But we have our independence. Hopefully things will get better," the other driver said.

"The Nippon have been driven out from this country," the stall owner mumbled while fanning herself.

My chest felt tight. I quietly took a deep breath.

"The Nippon are evil. They are liars. Claiming to be our elder brothers, they said they wanted to help us to get our independence and promised us a better life. Turned out they were oppressors, even crueler than the Dutch. Luckily they lost."

Matsumi was not cruel. She was kind, gentle, and sweet.

My heartache intensified.

Screaming children broke the silence of the sultry day. Disturbed by the noise, I turned my head. Several children chased each other in the temple yard, joking and laughing. They did not seem concerned with the volatile situation. War does not exist in a child's world. It is always full of color and laughter.

"The Chinese are better, like the people at the temple, for instance. They are willing to take in orphans," the owner said.

"More kids arrive every day. They are noisy. But then there's that quiet one, a pretty girl. She sits alone and doesn't play with others," the woman added.

"Why?" I joined the conversation just for fun. I thought it would help kill the time until night.

The woman shrugged her shoulders. "The other kids say she is a half mute," she laughed.

"Half mute?"

Still laughing, the woman continued. "The child never talks, but that doesn't mean she can't speak. She only talks with the old lady who takes care of the temple and an old gentleman who visits her every week. She doesn't understand Javanese or Chinese. Every day she sits there quietly, like she's waiting for someone."

That was a funny story. I chuckled and slowly exhaled.

"Who's the old gentleman? What language does she speak?"

The owner shrugged her shoulders again. "How should I know? She likes talking to the sun."

She shouted, "Oh, there she is. That's the girl."

"Pretty, isn't she?"

"Is she Chinese or Javanese?" asked the other man.

They continued talking about the child but I wasn't interested in a child who was half mute. It was more important to figure out where to go next to find Matsumi and Kaguya.

"A Dutch kid?"

"Well, she has black hair."

"Maybe Japanese."

"How could she be at the temple if she were Japanese? She would have been sent back to Japan."

This caught my attention. I threw a glance at the child, suddenly curious what she looked like. God knows why my heart was pounding.

Several children played and ran around the courtyard. But it was not difficult to spot the girl they were talking about. She sat by herself, squatting, and made scratches on the ground. Sometimes she looked up to the sky.

"That's the old Chinese gentleman who visits her every week," the owner whispered. "The girl waits for him. She rarely goes out to play in the courtyard."

I saw a man walking slowly toward the girl. He squatted besides her. Startled, she turned her head, and looked up to him. He held out a hand, apparently offering her something. When she burst out laughing, he rose. He reached for her and lifted her high above his head.

My heart pounded.

I used to do that to Kaguya, lifting her up high in the air and making her laugh out loud.

They spun around.

My vision blurred.

I felt dizzy.

The little girl was Kaguya.

I stood abruptly. Leaving my coffee and change on the table, I ran across the road toward the temple.

"Kaguya, Kaguya!" I shouted.

She turned her head toward me. "*Otosan*, Daddy. Otosan," the little girl screamed. She wriggled out of the old man's hold and ran to me.

Something exploded in my chest as I embraced her. I kissed her head and cheeks again and again. I was overwhelmed by mixed emotions.

"Where's Okasan?" I asked.

Kaguya shook her small head. Her round eyes blinked and became glazed, turning them into a pair of mirrors. Tears fell down her cheeks.

"Okasan," she sobbed.

Her cry pierced my heart. I knew something very sad had happened to make her cry with such pain.

The old gentleman, who had been watching, walked slowly to us.

"Are you Sujono?" he asked.

"How do you know, sir?"

"You are Kaguya's father," he said.

"Yes," I replied.

"Let us talk inside."

In the small office beside the temple, he introduced me to a middle-aged woman. Mama Nio was the caretaker of the temple. He introduced himself as Tuan Tan.

"Matsumi entrusted us with Kaguya," Mama Nio started the conversation.

"Where is she?" I asked.

"She has gone back to Japan," replied Tuan Tan.

My world turned upside down.

I was angry, sad, disappointed, and desperate. All these emotions were so mixed up that I could not tell which was the most important. I did not feel my feet touch the ground. My neck no longer seemed to support my head. My body could plunge to the ground at any time while my head flew into the sky.

"Matsumi did not have any other choice. It was best for her and Kaguya. This is only temporary. I'm sure that once things get better, Matsumi will come back for her," Mama Nio said.

Tuan Tan supported Mama Nio. "Matsumi really suffered. She told me much about her, you, and Kaguya. She couldn't continue to live here."

I could not deny what they said. Matsumi suffered much while living with me.

I was ashamed and looked at my little girl.

"I have to take Kaguya with me." I mumbled gravely. I was confused and did not know what to say. The desire to take Kaguya home was the only right thing to tell them.

The two Chinese people sighed almost simultaneously. As they exhaled, their breathing became heavy. They looked at each other in a way I did not understand.

"Do you want to take Kaguya with you?" Tuan Tan's voice was filled with doubt.

"Can you take good care of her?" Mama Nio asked in the same way.

"Matsumi entrusted Kaguya with us," Tuan Tan objected.

"We're responsible for Kaguya. We promised Matsumi to care for her," Mama Nio said.

They sounded as if they were competing to judge me. I detected an angry tone in their voices. Their words attacked me and made me feel useless. I could not support Matsumi and now I wanted to take Kaguya. What kind of life would I give her? That was the question they were asking.

They had said nothing wrong. Their words made me blush. However, any man would defend himself, especially when cornered.

"I am her father," I said, irritated. I was angry and ashamed. No matter what, I was Kaguya's father.

My outburst quieted both of them.

"I have the right to take Kaguya with me," I said, defensively.

Tuan Tan and Mama Nio exchanged doubtful glances.

"I'm the one who is responsible for Kaguya," I insisted firmly. It was obvious they would not let my child go.

Tuan Tan and Mama Nio took a deep breath. They were at a loss for words.

"It's true, you are her father. You have more rights than anyone to Kaguya and should be responsible for her life. But," Mama Nio softened her accusations.

"There's no but," I broke in.

Before I knew it, I had banged the table in front of me. The air tensed and we turned quiet. Tuan Tan broke the silence. "Where do you work?" he asked in a heavy tone.

His question stabbed me through the heart. This time I was unable to speak.

Seeing me quiet, the man saw a good opportunity to divert my anger.

"This country has only recently become independent. Things are as difficult as ever. Nothing meaningful has taken place. We're waiting for the new government to take the next step." He talked without giving me a chance to interrupt.

"Are you ready to take Kaguya with you in this trouble? That means you'll make her life difficult as well," he said, straight to the point. "You made Matsumi suffer. Do you want to subject Kaguya to the same ordeal?" he added more sharply.

I was dumbfounded. Tuan Tan made sense. My anger quieted and I began to understand the real situation rather than go into a rage propelled by hurt pride. If I took Kaguya with me, would I make the same mistake again?

Tuan Tan again implied that I did not have any choice but let Kaguya stay at the Hok An Kiong Temple. "If you care for her, do what Matsumi did and choose what is best for Kaguya."

But Kaguya held on to my hand tightly when I was about to say goodbye.

"Otosan is going home. I'll be back tomorrow," I said.

Kaguya shook her head violently. Tears welled up in her eyes. Her words were not clear yet.

"Otosan, want to come. Okasan, I want Okasan," she blubbered and cried.

Mama Nio helped me persuade Kaguya. She also looked teary, moved by what was happening. "Kaguya, stay here with Grandma Nio. Tomorrow your daddy will come back, and your mamma will be here soon to pick you up. Take a shower and change your clothes so you'll look pretty."

"I want to go with Otosan. I want Okasan. I don't want to stay here," Kaguya cried, lisping.

We tried to soothe her but she only cried more loudly.

Finally I freed my hand from her clutch and Mama Nio took Kaguya in her arms. The little girl struggled and shouted my name.

I hurried away.

"Otosan!" Kaguya's long cry cut through my insides. I hardened my heart and pretended to be deaf and blind. Matsumi might have had to do the same.

*****

After that meeting at Hok An Kiong Temple, I visited Kaguya every morning and late afternoon, but the situation worsened. Kaguya became ill and refused to eat, drink, or play. She did not want to speak. All she did was cry and sit dreamily waiting for me to come, and every time I left her, she would blubber, scream, and struggle. She became a sad child.

Mama Nio, Tuan Tan, and I tried hard to comfort Kaguya but the little girl only stared at us miserably. She did not say a single word and tears streamed down her face. She did not understand how difficult life was outside the temple. All she wanted was just to be with me, her father, as she did not know where to find her mother.

As Kaguya's condition worsened, we had to give in.

With Mama Nio and Tuan Tan's permission, I decided to take her to my small and stuffy room. I had often cursed the Chinese because they were notorious for being stingy, yet these people had helped my daughter. Mama Nio and Tuan Tan's generosity and humanity made them much richer than the Chinese who were only concerned with money. Not all of them were as bad as I thought. I owed them.

"From now on you have to work hard; you have Kaguya. She is your responsibility," Tuan Tan said, firmly and to the point. It made my ears burn. Matsumi must have told him a lot about me.

"Yes, I understand," I replied thoughtfully, feeling embarrassed.

"How about your wife? Have you talked to her about Kaguya? Would she mind Kaguya's presence? Will she be good to her?" Mama Nio bombarded me with questions.

I should have been offended; it was none of her business. I could have been angry with them for interfering in my personal life, but I accepted her words as she sounded very concerned about my daughter. I knew I would make a mistake no matter what I did. I could not deny that I had a hard life and did not know how Sulis would react to Kaguya. I did not have any idea about the kind of life I would give her.

I took a deep breath. The burden pressed on me. While I had been determined to find Kaguya and take her with me, I was now doubtful about my decision. Would this be good for her? It might be better for her to stay at the Hok An Kiong Temple.

There was the problem of not being able to buy food for our empty stomachs because I was unemployed, and there also was Sulis. The scorpion-faced woman appeared in my mind. How would she treat Kaguya? She was not a friendly person when faced with trouble. Poverty had sharpened her intuition to pick out new threats and she would do anything to keep them away. I was horrified at the thought of Sulis, and started to question my decision.

"I will care for and protect Kaguya no matter what happens. No one will hurt her and I'll do anything for her," I said, bitterly doubting myself.

Mama Nio and Tuan Tan stared at me quietly.

They knew me.

I was only Sujono, incapable of doing anything; I was useless.

"Hmm. It would be better if you found another name for Kaguya. Her name will attract too much attention in a kampung. This would be for her own good," Tuan Tan suggested carefully.

"Another name?" The thought only then occurred to me.

Kaguya could not use a Japanese name. It would invite too many questions in addition to the reasons for her living with us. Why add to the difficulties of my little girl? Would it not be better if I removed any possible problem?

I tried hard to think of a name as beautiful as Matsumi. I wanted to cherish my memory of her, and Kaguya was part of both of us.

"What about Lestari? She would be *lestari*, everlasting, for me and Matsumi."

"Lestari? That's a pretty name!" Mama Nio exclaimed.

"Lestari! Good," Tuan Tan laughed. He pinched Kaguya's cheek playfully and crooned, "Lestari, Lestari, you're very pretty."

I was moved seeing how much these Chinese people loved my daughter.

But what about Matsumi? The thought of her broke my heart. Was her disappointment in me so deep that it gave her the strength to leave Lestari, or was it the unbearable suffering I put her through? What would I do if Lestari looked for her? Could I raise the child? Life in the new republic was tough. Would Sulis be willing to share the rice basket with another mouth?

Ah, I thought of the infinite problems to solve and I did not need to explain further. If Matsumi had not suffered, she would not have left Lestari. It must have been beyond what she could bear that made her have the heart to do that. But how would I raise Lestari? I did not know. Our endless poverty made Sulis scream, opening her wide mouth even wider to fight over a spoon of rice.

I really did not know how I would manage.

Taking Lestari to our small room was like giving her a plate of raw suffering to chew and swallow. I felt this since the first time she set her foot in my home.

Sulis's tight frown pulled her two big eyes closer together and she glared at Lestari full of rejection. The corners of her wide mouth curved down like a bow, and her square jaw was set.

She was a scorpion ready to fight.

She sensed a new threat.

"This is Lestari. She's staying with us," I said, firmly. I did not explain who Lestari was, where she came from, or any of the sad details.

Sulis was neither dumb nor foolish. Poverty teaches us to defend ourselves. Sulis was smart enough to sense that life in our room was going to be different.

Her big mouth opened, her lips parted as if ready to devour prey. Her voice was deafening and her bulging eyes looked like they were going to jump out of their sockets. Sulis stood with one hand on her hip like a Dutch colonialist and pointed her finger at Lestari.

"Whose child is this? Why is she staying here? My God, you have lost your mind, Mas. Our life is already difficult and now you bring this child. Aren't we suffering enough?" Sulis shouted.

I used to like to fight. I liked to see Sulis hurt like she hurt my pride. I felt satisfied when she screamed in agony. I did not care when she finally learned how to get even. I really did not care. I was even glad to have a matching opponent.

But now there was Lestari, and I was reluctant to fight. I did not want her to hear Sulis's grumbling and see her scorpion face.

I just wanted Lestari to be comfortable. It was the only thing I thought about.

"Lestari won't trouble us," I replied while preparing a sleeping mat for her.

I spread out an old mat and covered it with a piece of ragged cloth. It was nothing like the warm futon she was used to, but at least my little girl did not have to lie on the cold floor.

Lestari turned out to be very troublesome that night. She cried all night, looking for Matsumi. She must have thought that she would see her mother if she came with me, but instead, I had given her another mother.

Lestari also did not like our tiny room. She was not used to sleeping on a cold floor in a hot and humid room with mosquitoes buzzing around. She usually slept on a warm and nice-smelling futon in Matsumi's arms while listening to her sweet lullabies.

Lestari refused to eat since we only had crusty cold rice with sweet soy sauce. Matsumi always fed her warm rice and tasty soup. She was also used to being spoon-fed by her mother, who did it while talking and joking with her.

I also knew that when she stayed at the Hok An Kiong Temple, Lestari was the pet of many people and never short on candy. She was well groomed and slept in the same bed as Mama Nio. While it was not as comfortable as when she was with her own mother, it was much better than being with the scorpion and me in our tiny room.

Lestari ran to the door and banged on it, trying to get out to perhaps look for Matsumi. She never stopped whining and crying.

I did not know what to do. I had never looked after a child.

"Okasan, Okasan," Lestari sobbed for Matsumi.

She also called for Mama Nio. "Grandma, Grandma."

She was like a chick that had lost its mother hen. Walking around the crowded room, she alternated pulling on me with running to the door. Sulis should have soothed her.

She could have held the child in her arms and rocked her while talking softly to comfort her, just the way Matsumi used to do. She could also have fed the little girl.

But she did not do either.

Sulis raged when she heard Lestari babble in Japanese. "What did she say? Did she speak Nippon? She's Nippon. Is she the Nippon slut's daughter, your illegitimate child? Why did you bring her here?"

I could not do much.

Lestari could not speak fluently yet—she still lisped. Besides, Matsumi also always spoke Japanese to her. I understood little of what she said and could not calm her.

"And what did you say? She won't trouble us? Look, she's a real bother. She makes this room even smaller. I cannot sleep because of her crying. She eats our rice. She's already too much trouble while she is young. What will happen when she grows up?" Sulis's words rolled out of her evil mouth.

"Get her out of here. I won't have her live with us." Sulis opened the door and with one hand on her hip, pointed outside. The night's cold air burst into the room. It was pitch black outside.

I realized that Sulis was not Matsumi. I could not expect any kindness from the scorpion.

Watching Sulis open the door and her finger pointing outside, Lestari stopped crying. She looked frightened. Perhaps she thought a monster had appeared, something very different from the angel who was usually with her. She crumpled and her face turned gray. Lestari waddled a few steps toward the looming darkness, and stopped. There was now a different fear in her innocent eyes. She looked at the blackness of the quiet, late night, confused. Maybe she wondered whether she would find a beautiful angel or a fiercer monster in the darkness.

She came back to me, submissive. She might not have understood what was going on but I was sure she knew she was going to get hurt.

"No. She must stay with us. She doesn't have anyone and doesn't know where to go," I said, irritated.

"That's not my problem. All I know is that she will add to our misery. And I'm not the Nippon slut's maid. If she could give birth to the child, she can take care of her. Get the little slut out of here," Sulis shouted, sending me a challenging look.

The people in the kampung must have pressed their ears against their walls to find out what was going on in my tiny room. On such a quiet night a dropped needle sounded like a cannon shot, let alone Sulis's screams. They would surely be busy talking about us tomorrow.

I held back my anger. It hurt me when I heard Sulis insult Lestari, but I did not do anything. I could have punched Sulis with my fist; I hated seeing her rude big eyes and her wide, always open mouth. I was satisfied when I saw the black and blue bruises appear on her body and face. I liked to give her such a lesson because it quieted her for several days, although she would be ready for a new attack soon after.

But I could not do so now since I did not want to be violent in front of Lestari. The girl was upset enough after crying all day for Matsumi. Her pretty eyes were filled with confusion and sadness and she looked tired. I did not want to frighten her by fighting like an animal with Sulis. I would not make her suffer like Matsumi.

Sulis smelled an advantage from my attitude. She grumbled and cursed all night while pouting and rolling her eyes. Her loud voice competed with Lestari's cries. She did not care; she bawled me out while pointing at Lestari and me. Sulis used Lestari to pour out her hatred for me, like she had a new toy to play with. Hurting me through my daughter pleased her.

Although Lestari did not understand what Sulis said, her intuition must have told her something was wrong. Sulis made her more upset and frightened.

Finally, she fell asleep in front of the door just before the sun appeared at *subuh*. She lay limp and tired after crying all night with an empty stomach. Her eyes were shut tight and swollen. Her chest moved up and down irregularly from unconscious sobbing. Her dirty face was covered with tracks of dried tears and snot.

Filled with rage, I lifted Lestari and slowly lay her besides me. I wiped the dried tears on her cheeks, and my eyes were warm and wet as I felt her suffering. I knew taking her to Sulis would be tough, but I had not expected it to be this terrible.

My chest hurt when I heard myself call for Matsumi inside my heart: Matsumi, where can you be? Kaguya is looking for you. She needs her mother.

The response was only the empty echo of my own voice.

But Sulis's voice was loud and clear.

"Where's the Nippon slut? Why did she leave you? Has she gone back to Japan? She's left the suffering to you. What did you expect of a whore? Once a slut, always a slut. You take care of the slut's daughter. Only an angel would do that."

She sounded very satisfied. I was usually in control of our fights, but now she had won. She smirked, happy she could hurt Lestari and tuck a burning coal in the child's little heart. I felt it, because the assault was meant for me.

Sulis never took care of Lestari. She refused to give her a shower and the girl who had always looked pretty and smelled nice turned into a filthy and shabby looking child.

Sulis let Lestari cry all day from hunger. She filled her own stomach before she let the child scrape the soft part of rice crusts. She let the two-year-old feed herself. When Lestari dropped food on the floor, Sulis roughly pulled the metal plate from her hands and hit the youngster in the mouth.

The plate's bottom cut the corner of her lips. Blood drizzled from the cut. Lestari screamed. She was obviously in pain.

"That's punishment for making the floor dirty." Sulis clearly enjoyed the girl's wailing.

To me, her words sounded like, "Look, I can make your child's mouth bleed just like you do to me."

There was much satisfaction and glory in each word she said.

I knew Sulis took out her anger toward me on Lestari. She also threw her hatred for Matsumi at the child. She had the heart to hurt a little girl like Lestari. Sulis often made up reasons to hurt Lestari while I was at work because she did not dare do it in front of me. I would not hesitate to hit her with my fists and give her the same bruises and cuts she put on my little girl. Although I tried to refrain from fighting with Sulis in front of Lestari, I could not help doing it when she had gone too far. But Sulis was a sly scorpion. She knew how much would be too much for me.

Knowing how much she had to suffer, my love for Lestari grew deeper. I got up early in the morning to give her a shower and feed her before leaving for work at the harbor. I did not want to see her dirty and starving, or for Sulis to hit her mouth with a plate. I always came home with cassava or fried banana because I knew she would not have had enough food.

Since I did not want Lestari to lack anything, I no longer worked only when I felt like it. I was willing to do any work to fulfill her needs and smoked fewer cigarettes to buy her a bag of candy. I liked seeing her happy after waiting for me at the door of our room and jumping up gleefully when I gave her the candy.

My love for Lestari was not the same as my feeling toward Joko. I never loved him like I loved her. I always put her needs before his, not because she was my daughter or because Sulis always mistreated her, but because she was Matsumi's daughter. I loved that woman very much.

I always hoped that one day Matsumi would return to Indonesia and look for Lestari and me. I could not give her anything when she lived with me, even though she had given up her rich world where she never lacked anything. I had adored her too much, and loved her too much. I had been too selfish and I did not deserve her. What I did was drown her in a long suffering.

Now I wanted to prove that I could be responsible. I wanted to show Matsumi I could raise Lestari properly. Although I was poor, I would do my best, according to my feelings and abilities.

But...

Was I wrong in saying that I loved her too much?

Did she know how much I loved her?

Did she know how miserable I was after she left me?

I could only prove my love to her when she saw how I had looked after and raised Lestari.

Every day, I expressed my longing for her by looking at the sun. Matsumi had come from the sun and returned to it. The sun never breaks its promises. While it always disappears and leaves darkness behind, it also returns and shines again the next morning.

Missing Matsumi made me feel hollow and hurt me deeply.

Matsumi will definitely come back.

I will wait for her, forever.

Part 5: Lestari

Kyoto, December 2003

I have suffered too long and no longer weep.
Time has silenced my voice.

Maya and Higashi were married in early December 2003, in Surabaya. I gave a small party in the middle room of our orphanage. Although simple, it was lively and moving.

Maya looked pretty in her simple-cut ivory wedding gown and a tiara holding her black hair. Little roses were scattered over the train of her dress.

A wedding gown? Tears came to my eyes seeing Maya wearing hers. Every girl dreams of meeting her prince with a smile, looking as beautiful and elegant as Cinderella, and holding hands with him while walking toward the future. I never had that kind of dream. Severe injuries had scarred my cheeks and also destroyed my hopes. My dreams were always dark and my world was colorless. I had lost my smile and did not talk much. Never did I allow a man to approach me or peek into my heart.

Once, in a short, unfinished dream, a young prince offered me flowers as a token of love. He wanted to kiss me but my wedding dress dissolved and I stood suddenly alone. The handsome prince stayed stuck between my eyelashes. He came and went as I blinked from sleeping to waking. He never became real.

In another dream, the prince turned into a two-faced grimacing wolf. He brought me neither love nor flowers, and forced me to eat a poisonous apple. He was very cruel. He clawed my entire body until I lay limp, covered in blood.

I woke up gasping to get rid of the dream. There seemed to be no difference between being awake and asleep; the wound was still there. So I let my life become dark like the night. I tried to feel my way and hide my bleeding wounds. I wanted to forget the man-wolf and did not understand why he chased me from one night to the next.

I did not dare to call for the handsome prince who had brought me flowers and love. I was afraid my wedding gown would be torn from my body, leaving me naked.

I was ashamed.

And the shame was very painful.

In my life, Father was the only man who gave all his love to me. He knew of my secret pains and wounds. We never talked about the wounds anymore. Father knew I wanted to forget them. Isn't time the best way to forget?

Father often mistreated the evil woman who lived with us. They fought everyday. I always triggered their fights. The woman hated me very much. In the end, Father removed me from the hell she had created.

"We're leaving this place. I won't let her hurt you any more. We're going to Matsumi's house. That's where you belong," Father said as we left.

I do not remember anything else he said. At that time words lost their meaning and my mind filled with somber colors. I searched for other colors and did not find any. Even white looked like soot.

Over time, my face became empty and I did not see anything in front of me. My tongue hung out of my mouth like a thirsty dog out of breath from running. It felt as if it had been stretched to my chin and I was unable to pull it back. I wanted to scream but I knew I would not be heard and my tongue froze. I wanted to howl like a dog because of my unbearable pain but I was in such agony I did not utter a sound. My sobs kept me from speaking the many words and feelings that lay on the tip of my tongue. Every night I woke with a sudden pain in my chest. I did not cry, only gasped for breath.

When I first entered Matsumi's house, I was enveloped in warmth emanating from a sense of peace and comfort. My battered body and soul were refreshed. Somehow, my soul was connected to the house through time.

The experience was similar to opening an old dusty book. As I turned the pages, dust motes made me sneeze and made my hair dirty. I was thrown into the past; a sunset with a purple sky. I was lifted high into the sky and reached with both hands for the yellow moon as it waned like melting butter.

A pleasant fragrance wafted from each corner of the house. Paintings that depicted morning, noon, and night told me stories. I felt the breeze and the warmth of the sun coming through the window frames. I heard whispers.

I reached out and there was nothing. I searched for the warmth by inhaling as much air as possible. The warmth crept through my veins. My blood started flowing again, and my heart beat. I ran between the front and the rear of the house. I walked into every room. I jumped into the yard and rolled on the lawn. I picked up every image scattered around the house of a woman laughing, fragrant hair, a hug against a warm chest, sweet lullabies, and gentle strokes on the forehead. These images of the past were everywhere. But the images were incomplete, only fragments that appeared briefly and vanished almost immediately. The corners of my eyes were wet. Tears streamed down my cheeks and I could not make a sound; my chest and shoulders quivered.

"Lestari, we'll stay here until Matsumi returns to find you. We'll wait here for her." Father's words echoed in my ear.

Matsumi? Why should we have to wait for her? From where would she return? Who is she?

I always had many questions when hearing that name. Father always mentioned it with lots of emotion and hope; he had love and pain in his voice and eyes when he spoke of Matsumi. He lived each day with hope of her return.

Every time he took a breath, there was yearning in the air he inhaled and exhaled. He said her name before he died.

Why did Matsumi mean so much to him?

Strangely, I also felt a connection to the name, as if it lived in my heart. It caused a longing to rush through my blood. I felt the spirit of a wandering soul looking for me.

What was going on?

Just when my longing had reached the breaking point, Matsumi stood in front of me. My dream came true when I was already very tired of waiting. She became reality as Higashi's adoptive mother, and Maya's mother in-law.

She was not a shadow in a dream. She was real.

Matsumi was the woman who had given birth to me. She was the woman who had left me.

I was lost for words when she lifted the dark veil that Father had hidden the past under until he died. I did not know whether to cry or be happy at finding the woman in whose womb I had lived warmly for nine months. I did not know whether to be angry or disappointed at facing the woman who left me. She had poisoned my life for more than fifty years.

How could I find the connection between mother and daughter that was lost for so long? For years I had searched and waited for her with so much longing, but now I only had a sense of strangeness when we looked into each other's eyes.

*****

Several weeks after the wedding, Higashi took Maya to Kyoto. Matsumi and Maya asked me to live with them in Japan, but I could not leave the orphanage I had run for decades. There was too much baby blabber and laughter I could not leave. The house had become part of my soul.

However, in the end, I went along and visited Kyoto with Higashi and Maya before they left for their honeymoon.

Matsumi invited me to stay at her ryokan, the traditional Japanese inn she owned. I called her "Okasan" afterward.

The inn was lovely. The landscaping included a rock garden and a pebble footpath. Bonsais of pine, bamboo, and plum filled the corners. Across from where we sat was a water fountain made of several tiered clay pots. The water flowed from a bamboo pipe and made a trickling sound.

We sat on tatami mats spread on the wooden floor. We had taken off our sandals before entering the room and sat across from each other with a short-legged table between us. The sliding door stayed open so I could enjoy the lovely garden view.

I sat cross-legged in front of Okasan. I watched her wrinkled hands reach for several stalks of flowers and arrange the stems gracefully into a vase so their heights became one and a half times the vase's height. She added nine other stalks of different flowers in various positions, some straight up, others bending.

Matsumi was almost eighty years old but still healthy. She was a vegetarian. Every day she walked to the shrine for prayer. Her body had kept its shape. Although her skin was wrinkled, it looked soft and clean. Her silver hair was always tidily combed. She looked younger than her age.

I felt strange sitting in front of my biological mother. Was it because I had suffered alone for too long? Or had I become used to living without a mother and lost hope of ever seeing her again? Could it have been because of the lack of love or affection between us?

I felt awkward sitting in front of her.

Matsumi's soft, gentle voice broke the silence in spare and halting Indonesian. "Kaguya, this is *ikebana*—the art of arranging flowers. The *rikha* style has been known since the fifteenth century in Kyoto. This style uses nine stalks. We arrange them in a specific way to create a harmony and balance."

She called me Kaguya.

The name sounded foreign, but I could not help noticing the refreshing effect her voice had on my soul that had been barren for decades. My intuition could not deny that it was Okasan's voice I had longed for. Hers was the voice I had searched for in my dark dreams. It sounded like trickling water with a beautiful melody, calm like the gentle breeze and soothing.

I had yearned for her voice for decades, looking in the darkness and loneliness of my early childhood. But all I heard in the tiny room where I lived with Father were the curses of a woman I called "Mother," and who called me a little slut.

Just when I had become used to living without the voice, when I had learned to enjoy my dull life and stopped searching, the voice was suddenly present, right in front of me.

My eyes stung.

I trembled.

My chest was tight.

I hated the woman in front of me. She gave birth to me but never wanted me as her child. I was hurt because she abandoned me.

"You could have learned ikebana if I had taken you with me," Matsumi's voice drifted.

I heard the guilt in her bitter tone. She tempered my anger, cooled my rage, and muffled my disappointment. It lightened my heart that she spoke Indonesian, even while living so far away.

"The situation did not allow this. After the Japanese surrendered to the Allies, Japanese people were detained and shipped back to their home country. The trip took months.

"A Chinese man helped me get out of Surabaya on a Chinese commercial ship. I left the city not as Japanese but Chinese, since my documents identified me as Tjoa Kim Hwa. I had used that name to enter Indonesia. I was not treated as a prisoner of war, but the suffering was no less. I wandered around in the ship tired, hungry, scared, and restless. I had no food or money. A storm almost crashed our ship and pirates robbed us in the middle of nowhere. They took all the ship's goods and I had nothing left but the clothes I wore. I no longer knew if I was alive or dead.

"The ship reached China in winter. Chinese winters are so severe that the cold penetrates the bones. I only had the old clothes I wore and the journey home was still long. I had to catch a train to Pusan, Korea, and travel from that station on to Japan. But heavy snow covered the rails to Pusan.

"The train could not run and they made me get off and help shovel snow off the rails because I was only hitchhiking. The biting cold hardened my tender hands. They were no longer pale but bluish and the blood seemed to freeze. When I was thirsty and hungry, I picked up a lump of snow and sucked on it to fill my stomach.

"When I finally arrived in Japan, life was still tough. Japan was destroyed. The country was in chaos with no signs of life, only sadness.

"It was not possible to take you with me under those conditions. Not only because you did not have identification papers but also because of the unbearable suffering. The journey was not meant for a two year-old girl.

"I should have stayed in Surabaya. I had you, didn't I? But I don't think I would have been able to survive. My life with Sujono wasn't what I expected: he still had a wife and son to support and did not work. He was jealous, lazy, and abusive. He did not let me return to the club in Kembang Jepun although you were already born and we were short of money. He did not treat me with respect. I was tortured and humiliated every day. He loved me in his own peculiar way. He did not give me a sense of comfort and peace." Matsumi ended her story with bitterness.

Listening to what she had to say was difficult. Matsumi talked bad about Father while he really loved her. He had accepted the grief that made his life miserable, but then I was too naive to understand the depth of their love. I wanted to defend him but didn't know how. Even now I knew too little about love to talk about it. I never had a lover or husband. Okasan knew much more about men and women than I did.

"Kaguya, it is a miracle we are here today. When I look back, an extraordinary strength must have enabled me to carry on. I never thought we could be together again. How great life is.

"Do you know how much I ached when I had to leave you in Surabaya? I loved you, but the years after the war were very hard. There was no other choice; you had to remain in Indonesia." She continued with a heavy sigh. "It's fine if you hate me. It was my fault. A mother should not leave her child. I'm always haunted by guilt. In Japanese we say, *gomen nasai*, I'm sorry," Matsumi stammered. She bowed, tears filling her eyes.

She behaved like a sinner confessing to her priest or a prisoner who had accepted the death penalty and was ready to be executed. She looked weak and did not defend herself.

With me in front of her, her glassy eyes seemed to mirror my reflection. Why had I become so cold and hard? I saw myself as a judge about to drop the gavel, a hangman ready to drop an offender, an executioner about to swing his ax.

"*Gomen nasai, gomen nasai,* I've made you suffer all this time," Matsumi repeated her apologies as if she had nothing else to say.

Was I satisfied?

Had I punished her enough with my silence?

I licked my dry lips; my eyes were warm and glazed. I gritted my teeth and bit my lips to control the turmoil inside. I was unable to sort out what I felt.

"It's fine, Okasan. Father was very good to me and loved me very much," I finally answered with uncertainty in my raspy voice. I tried to hold back my tears and control the strong waves in my heart.

My reply really favored Father. I still wanted to punish her. Although I knew how much she hated him, I remained on his side. This was normal and proper. She had left and only he stayed with me.

I knew telling her about my love for Father would hurt her and I was happy to have this power. It felt good to see her cry since she had hurt me for decades and made me unable to cry. Did I want to take revenge? But I did not see anger in her. Instead, she asked sadly, "How about Sujono's wife? How did she treat you?"

Her question silenced me.

I had wanted to hurt her but I was hurt instead. I sobbed. My tongue stiffened. I could not speak a single word.

"How did she treat you?" Matsumi repeated. The question tore at the veil I had used to cover my wounds. I could no longer shoulder the burden I had carried for more than fifty years and started to tell my story. My voice was hoarse; I was no longer able to refrain from crying. Tears streamed down my cheeks, although before I had only allowed my eyes to be moist like the dew before it vanishes in the sunlight. I swallowed and told her about living in Father's home.

"When I first entered the tiny room, I knew the woman I was supposed to call Mother did not like me. She always scowled, and glared at me with hatred while she nagged. She not only cursed me, she starved me, beat me across the mouth with a tin plate, and humiliated me. She never called me Lestari.

"She called me a little slut," I hollered like a wounded lion. The incidents should never be mentioned but the time had come to reveal them.

I continued my story of sorrow. It was about wounds, deep wounds, and wide wounds.

About getting hurt, deeply and intensely. I wanted to forget everything but I couldn't.

I could no longer hold back my yearning to talk with the woman who had given birth to me. I became like a blubbering child telling her mother that a friend had pinched her. I poured out all my longing to her, my pains of being abandoned and my loneliness from living by myself.

I told Matsumi about my bleak childhood. "There was no laughter or affection from Mother. I cringed in a corner of the room or in the toilet crying and frightened because of Mother standing with a hand on her hip and pointing her finger at me. Her big mouth cursed like a gun spewing bullets. Worse, she also threw and slammed whatever she found while yelling so loud the whole kampung talked about her.

"I never played since I had to do all the house chores. If I did not sweep the floor or boil water, I would not get any rice. I starved until Father returned from work at the harbor. Pinching, beating, hair pulling, and slaps with the tin plate were all part of my day. Blood flowed down the corner of my lips and dribbled into my rice, but I enjoyed it like a sweet soy sauce since I did not have anything else to eat. The cut did not feel painful afterward. It hurt more when she called me a little slut.

"Only Father gave me comfort. He always put my needs above everything else. He was willing not to smoke and work overtime just so he could buy me candy.

"He always said, 'I hope your life will be sweet.'

"Of course, that became the focus of Father and Mother's fighting from morning to night. I hunched on a corner of my thin mat like a wet mouse while she pointed her finger at me and shouted, 'Mas, you favor the little slut over your own child.'

"'Don't say that. Lestari's my daughter,' Father replied.

"'Oh, I see. Isn't Joko your son? The little slut is your illegitimate child with the Nippon whore. All the kampung people already know. Her mother is a tart, and she'll be one when she is a bit older. You're taking care of a baby lion. But Joko is your son. You should give him more attention than the little whore. Joko isn't a baby lion. He will take care of you until you die,' she said.

"Then, wide-eyed, she pointed her finger at me. 'You're a little slut. You're the Nippon whore's daughter. The whore stole my husband from me and now you're making trouble for us. You won't be much different from your mother when you grow up. Slut. Whore.'

"She poured the abuse like a bucket of water over my head."

I shook from remembering. Should I have swallowed the insults? I did not know the meaning of the words "slut" and "whore." I wanted to spit them out; they tasted bitter.

When Mother said, "You won't be much different from your mother," did it mean she was not my mother? Where was my mother? Where had she been? Why was she quiet and didn't defend me? I wanted to be deaf, unable to hear anything.

I continued. "Using the back of his strong hand, Father slapped Mother and bruised her cheek. 'Don't say that to Lestari. Don't hurt her heart.'

"Mother cried, screamed, and cursed. Of course, the scene was accompanied by door slamming, tin cups flying, and clothing thrown about. She created a big commotion. Her teary eyes were full of vengeance and hatred when she glared at me. She looked cruel; she was like a demon.

"I knew what would happen on the following day while father was at work. The woman would punch and scratch me, but I was already used to it."

Okasan furrowed her forehead while she listened. She looked surprised.

"How could it have come to that?" she said, in disbelief.

"Oh, that was nothing."

My heart beat louder, and I tried to blink away the tears running down my cheeks.

Wiping my wet cheeks I felt the long scars.

Okasan asked with a mother's sad voice, "What happened to your face?"

She reached out to feel my cheeks. Her gentle touch caressed them. Her hand felt cool on my scars that were still hot from the burning coal of Mother's hatred.

I felt the long scars. They stretched from my temple to near the lips, and were very deep. More than three thick lines of scars marred my face. They had shrunk my soul and robbed me of any confidence. They were just as painful as the hurtful words fixed in my mind:

"You're a Nippon whore's daughter. You're a tease like her. Your eyes are wild, seductive, lewd, and lustful when you look at a man."

Those were the curses Mother threw at me.

Her words were painful.

They tore me apart.

A real mother sang to her daughter, rocking, caressing, stroking, and kissing her with all her love. She spoke gently to her, comforting and praising her. She held her daughter's head in her hands and pulled her against her chest. She asked the moon to accompany her daughter's dreams and plucked the stars for her to play with. She built a palace for her sweetheart. A real mother was like the sun.

But my mother wounded my soul and stripped my dignity so I felt worthless and despicable. She hated me.

She was like an eclipse. She was a big-mouthed evil giant who swallowed the sun of my world and caused darkness to rule.

I grew up into what other people called a beautiful teenager, but with a gloomy face. I rarely smiled and did not dare look people in the eye. I always looked down. My eyes had no sparkle and I had no strength. I was imprisoned in a dark cell Mother had created for me.

Her abusive words rang in my ears and cut deep into my heart—I did not have the courage to fall in love. I could not look at men and open my heart to them.

I told Okasan, "As a teenager, I noticed the differences between my older brother, Joko, and me. My skin was light with yellow underneath while his was dark. My hair was straight while his was curly and coarse. My face did not look like Mother's, but his was a copy of hers. I did not look like a Javanese girl—only my eyes looked Javanese; they were round and had wide lids.

"Boys liked my light skin, round eyes, pointed nose, and shapely lips. They approached me, including Joko, my stepbrother.

"The room where we lived was tiny and limited our movement, especially when I was a teenager. The four of us slept together on the floor. The hot air became humid and even our breath sounded noisy. In the middle of the night, I could hear Father panting, the noise of a shifting mat, and Mother's long sighs.

"I did not know what they were doing and dared not open my eyes to peek at what was going on. I huddled and turned over to face the wall. I thought they were not finished yet with their fight. I did not understand why adults fought in the morning and wrestled naked with each other at night.

"The bathroom we used did not have a door. It was surrounded with a chest-high wall. After my breasts started to grow and I had my first period, I was reluctant to shower naked and seen by other people. I still did not understand about being a woman. No one told me about it and I did not ask Mother. Only my intuition told me my body was changing.

"I often caught Joko looking at me out of the corner of his eye. He tried to watch me while I showered. His wild looks undressed me and when Father and Mother were not home, he tried to touch me. I never was bold enough to tell Father since I knew it would make him quarrel with Mother, and afterward she would slap, scratch, and curse me.

"One day, I was changing clothes behind the wardrobe's door I had left open to cover my naked body after a shower. The tiny room was quiet. Father was at work and Mother, who usually sat around chatting with neighbors, was not there. God knew where she had gone. I did not see Joko anywhere either.

"All of a sudden Joko crashed into the room. Startled, I wrapped a kain around my growing breasts, but Joko jerked it away. I stood stark naked in front of him.

"Joko pushed and shoved me down. I struggled to free myself but I was too weak to fight him. He thrust something between my thighs. It was painful and made me sore. I felt warmth and then blood spotted the floor.

"It happened very quickly, in less than a minute. It was like an unfinished dream, and I was shocked when I realized a disaster had just struck my life. I felt very sore but the pain, the agony, not only came from my bleeding body."

Tears filled my chest, all my pores and flowed from the deepest corners of my heart. I could still see Joko grinning like a wolf, the wild, satisfied look in his eyes, but I could not describe his expression because what I had seen was too horrifying.

I continued. "Soon after, Mother came home. Her eyes popped when she saw me disheveled and naked standing next to the patches of blood on the floor. Her big mouth opened and closed like one of the fish I often saw at the river's edge, but her eyes glared like those of a fierce lion ready to pounce on his prey."

Pitiless. I shuddered from reliving the incident.

"What have you done to my son?" she shouted.

The question confused me. I did not how to answer. I was naked and bleeding and she could see I was pale, hurt, scared, and crying. She should have asked, "What has my son done to you?"

I had hardly overcome my confusion when she furiously pulled my hair and slammed my head against the wall repeatedly. Unsatisfied, she jerked my face up, and with a movement quicker than lightning she scratched my cheeks. She dug her long nails into my flesh and ran them across my face until I bled.

That, too, was not enough to release her anger. She grabbed a rusty, crooked fork. Holding my hair with one hand, she forced me to look up while she scraped the fork over my face. "No, please, Mother! Have mercy on me, Mother!" I howled in pain.

She seemed to enjoy my screams and seeing my agony.

"A little slut indeed. A flirt. A tart. You think you're pretty, don't you? You're still young but you tempt men already. Feel this. Let everyone know how beautiful and inviting you are. Take this for your flirting. Let me see how much your pretty face can attract men."

She scraped my cheeks again, again, and again, like she was removing the seeds from a cantaloupe.

"You have the talent to become a slut like your mother. She took my husband and now you're taking my son." The woman I called Mother grabbed my hair until she pulled out a handful.

"Nothing left to damage," she smirked. She looked happy at my wailing. Her grin no longer looked like that of a demon, but of a hellish demon; a demon-possessed demon.

She threw away the pile of hair and turned my face up. I trembled as I looked into her eyes. Inside were an inferno, thunder, a storm, trash, blood, and the crooked fork. Oh, and even more: an evil eye as huge as a ball, a headless Satan, a walking skeleton, a *kuntilanak,* the ghost with a hole in her back, a laughing ghost, a demon's tongue that stuck out and dripped saliva, and an eternal hell. I could not stand them; they scared me and I shut my eyes.

Then I felt something sticky squirt over my face, making it wet, maybe tears or blood, I thought.

She spit at me.

Once, twice, three times, again and again.

"Hey you little slut, you're really beautiful now. Argh."

I cried and cringed full of terror in a corner until Father returned. I quivered like a baby chick in an eagle's claws. My eyes were swollen and bruised and my stomach cramped. Mother's saliva still stuck to my face and hair and the scratches bled.

Not only did my cheeks bleed, my heart did too.

The woman I called Mother did not care about my condition. She acted like nothing had happened. Instead, she took care of her son who had pressed his body on me and hurt me. I even heard her tell him to make up a story.

"Tell Father the little slut tempted you when I was not home. She deliberately took off her clothes and seduced you."

I faintly heard her. Was she really my mother? Why did she hate me so much? I believed a real mother would have compassion for her daughter's sadness; why did she cut wounds in my heart instead? A real mother would be gentle to her child; why was she so cruel to me?

Was that woman not really my mother? Why did she always call me a little slut? What did it mean? Didn't she know my name was Lestari? Why had she never called me by that name? Wasn't it a pretty name?

So where was my real mother? Why didn't she protect me, look after me, and comfort and defend me?

I wept for having lost my mother and resumed telling my story.

"When Father came home, he was shocked when he saw me bleeding and a big war was inevitable.

"He beat Joko until his mouth, cheeks, and temples bled. He battered him like Mother had tortured me. He punched and kicked, and stomped his face, chest, and stomach until he lay in a limp heap. His eyes were swollen and blue and his face covered with blood.

"Mother screamed in his defense. 'The little slut has caused this. She's brought bad luck. She's a whore. You get out of here. Go away. Go! Go!'

"She put her hands on her hips like she usually did, and then pulled my lame body to the front door. She tried to throw me out of the room like a pile of rubbish.

"I slumped as she pulled me.

"Father freed me from her hands. 'You get out of here, not her,' he said. He pushed until Mother fell and her cruel face hit the floor. He then dragged her to the door as if he was going to throw out a dead mouse. She wriggled, trying to free herself. Her hands reached for anything she could grip, including the door, to stop him from dragging her.

"Father went wild. He trampled and kicked her repeatedly but she hunched over and tightly clutched the doorframe. Finally he grabbed her hair. Pulling it to get her outside, he plucked a bunch from her scalp.

"She let out a long painful howl. The voice did not come from her throat but from all the beings in hell that rumbled together to crash into the heavens.

"The kampung was in an uproar.

"People came running and scrambled to hold Father and help Mother, Joko, and me."

Was it necessary to help me? Even the angels could not help.

"With flaming eyes, Father poked his finger at Mother's forehead. 'Never show me your face again if you don't want to die,' he said. But the fire also burned in her eyes. She did not cry, although her face was wet with tears from an overwhelming hatred that desired murder. She looked like a thick-skinned crocodile with small eyes that blinked and shed tears as it gobbled its prey."

As I told her my memories, I could not help crying in front of Okasan. Tears rushed between my fingers, the tears I had kept to myself for years poured out like from a bursting dam. I blubbered like a small child.

Mother was indeed a crocodile.

One that swallowed the sun.

Since then, the dream haunted my sleep every night. It was as if I could never wake up from that nightmare.

It continued grinding and grinding.

I trembled.

I wriggled.

I crashed.

A flood of blood.

I cramped and convulsed until my tongue hung down my chin, rigid.

The crocodile had devoured the sun.

Hell.

*****

Now I had found my mother, I poured out my terrible past. My real mother felt for my heartaches and injuries; any mother cried when her child cried and laughed when her child laughed. It is never too late to cry in front of one's mother. After living for years like a thirsty pilgrim, I finally found an oasis in my mother.

Okasan's tears streamed down as she listened to me. We cried and hugged each other. We shared the wounds inflicted over other wounds.

"*Gomen nasai*, forgive me. It was my mistake," Matsumi repeated. "Kaguya, it wouldn't have happened if I had kept you with me. I've done you wrong. I have sinned." She wept, her lips trembling.

I took a deep breath and gasped. The tumult in my chest raged after I exposed the darkest part of my life. It felt as if a burden weighing more than a thousand tons had been lifted from me.

"Is that why you never married?" Okasan asked, sobbing.

I did not answer the question. It would only make my bleeding wounds hurt more. While the wounds would always be there, they would scab with time.

During the thick silence that followed we were left with our tears drying on our cheeks. After that, as if we had agreed, Okasan never talked about the scars on my face. It was like what I did with Father. We all had the same word in mind: forget. And there was only one way to forget, and that was not talk about it. And time would help us.

Maybe I could forget what happened to me, but I would not forget Father. He was the only man in my life. I did not know how he had loved or hurt Okasan, but I knew his love for her was very deep. He carried this love filled with regrets until his last breath.

I wanted her to know about him, and his love. I returned to my story.

"After what happened, Father took me from the tenement. I was feverish and trembling but we still moved out. He was furious at Mother and Joko. While he always treated them rough, he had never spoken of leaving them. But now he walked away without looking back.

"Mother screamed at him to stay. I thought she was scared of losing him, not because she loved Father since she had never treated him well, but out of her fear of poverty. He was the only one who worked. All she did was attack him.

"I was extraordinarily relieved at leaving that room full of nightmares. Father took me right away to an empty house he called Matsumi's house. He said it had been empty for a long time and he had locked it up but sometimes still swept the floors. He said Matsumi's house was my house, but he never told me who you were or explained how we were related. He just said to wait for you in the house. He was certain of your return and then I would know you.

"He took care of me in that house. I was sick for a long time and did nothing but cry. I was haunted by nightmares and refused to talk. But I liked to sit on the verandah to watch the sunrise and sunset. Father often sat with me, talking to me and telling me about the sun, about its promise to rise again after leaving the sky every day."

"And?" Okasan's voice was flat and cold.

I continued. "I liked the house. It was shady, comfortable, and warm. I felt as I had lived there before. Days turned into months, and months into years. We spent all of our time there until I turned into an adult and Father became old. It was lonely with just the two of us and I decided to take in abandoned and orphaned babies. As time passed the babies we cared for increased in numbers. Matsumi's house filled with their cries and babbles. The place was no longer quiet. It made me happy to give the homeless a home, especially since I was one of them. Maya was also abandoned.

"That's how your house became known as an orphanage, where abandoned babies are warmly welcomed."

For a moment a heavy, painful silence fell between us. The only sound was our breathing as it mingled with the wind.

"Father worked hard to provide for our daily needs and my education. He did odd jobs, day and night. He worked as a coolie at Tanjung Perak Port, and as a pedicab driver for extra income. He changed a lot. As far back as I remember, he and Mother quarreled because he never made enough money. She always said he never took his work seriously. But when it was only the two of us, we never lacked anything. He always took very good care of me."

"Oh, good." Okasan's voice was cold.

"Father worked day and night, sometimes even to dawn. I often saw blisters on his shoulders that were calloused from carrying heavy loads at the harbor. He had a heavy cough from working into the early hours of the morning and his smoking habit. I often said he should take a rest and smoke less but he always said he was fine. Working hard, he could meet our needs. He said he wanted Matsumi to know he had taken care of me. And he enjoyed his cigarettes. It was like he could see her image in the plumes of smoke.

"Near the end he had a stroke that paralyzed him and put him in a wheelchair. Later he was diagnosed with stage-four lung cancer that was impossible to cure; the cancer cells had spread to his throat and vocal cords. He was unable to speak clearly and had to eat and drink through a small hole the doctors made in his throat. But he had a few things he loved to do that never changed. He loved to make orisurus and watch the sun. He always longed for Matsumi; hers was the only name he said until the end of his life. He always wanted to see Matsumi again. But his dream never came true." My chest hurt as I ended my story.

Okasan looked thoughtful but I found it difficult to read her face. Her eyes were blurred and flat like a bottomless well.

I wondered if she had any feeling for Father, be it love, longing, disappointment, or hatred. He had yearned for her until his death. Her name was engraved on his heart. Had he hurt her so much that she did not have any feeling left for him?

Had she done what I did, kept the wounds to herself? Or had she forgotten them because she could not forgive? She did not seem interested in opening that gloomy chapter of her past. I guess that she did not know where to store the memories and decided to leave them alone, and let time bury them for her.

I was miserable. Why did both of us have a dark past? It made us hide many things. While other people were like open books anyone could read, we were like firmly locked diaries with torn pages left in a dark corner, accumulating dust.

Our eyes met. If eyes are really the windows to the soul, hers had no room for Father. He may have been a pile of dust that dirtied the pages of her book. She had torn out the pages and discarded them. She did not want to look back.

A cold silence fell between us. It was as if only our hearts could speak of the pain, loneliness, and wounds.

Okasan heaved a long sigh. In a flat tone, she said, "Kaguya, it's in the past. Life is not always about looking back; to the contrary, it is about moving forward. There's nothing to blame, and nothing to remember. All that happens is Life's game and we are only players. We don't know what Life holds for us.

"When I returned to Kyoto in 1945, I did not know what to do or where to go. It was impossible to return to my village; it was just a poor area. Meanwhile I was penniless. I did not know where to find work because the situation in Japan was awful after its defeat. Hiroshima and Nagasaki were destroyed. The economy was in chaos. Many factories were shut down and there was unemployment everywhere.

"With little hope, I went to Gion to look for Yuriko-san. I hoped she would at least be able to give me a place to sleep until I found work. She received me with open arms. Filled with remorse, I told her how much I had suffered with Sujono. She did not insult or blame me, but she regretted I had abandoned you, Kaguya." Matsumi paused.

"Not only Yuriko-san, but anyone who knew I had left my child behind would criticize me. I was not a good mother." Matsumi ended with a hollow laugh. She looked at me. "Do you know what I felt?"

I shook my head and waited for her to speak.

"I hated Sujono very much. He made me worthless, very low, despicable, because he caused me to be an irresponsible mother.

"I cursed him with everything I had. I hated him with every breath I took. I didn't blame him for what had gone wrong. No, I just hated that I had fallen in love with him. I hated having trusted him. I hated having given birth to his child. I hated that my sacrifices turned out to be useless. I hated my foolishness. I hated myself."

I was shocked.

Matsumi had so far appeared calm, almost without feeling, but now she raged with hate. Her eyes blazed. She squinted in pain and pressed her lips tightly together. A crystal-like shadow appeared in her eyes and melted into drops of water that ran down her wrinkled face.

Were those tears of pain, or hatred, or regret? I had no idea.

"I vowed that I would never cry over Sujono again," Matsumi said. She wiped her cheeks quickly with the back of her hand. "I have cried too much for the wrong man," she added.

Her voice was steady again. How quickly she gained control of her emotions. I knew now she did not have any feeling left for Father. He had no place in her heart, not even as an object of hatred or disappointment. The flat tone of her voice and the cold expression in her eyes said everything. It was as though she never had held his name in her heart or cherished his love.

I knew how much Father had pined for her. I had watched his yearning thicken and crystallize until he died. He had waited for Matsumi throughout his life. He only shared his longing with the sun and talked about it with his paper cranes. All he hoped for was to see her again.

Perhaps there is truth in the words of a poet that claimed love and hate to be as thin as an onionskin. Are they like two sides of the same coin that can be turned at anytime? Can hate instantly turn into love, and can love suddenly turn into hate?

Okasan's voice broke into my conflicting thoughts. "There's a shrine on Shijo Street in the eastern part of Gion. I often went there to pray when I was a teenager. When I returned to Kyoto, I went there right away to pray for you, Kaguya.

"One day after I finished praying, a man approached me and introduced himself. His name was Takeda; he was a painter. He asked if I would be willing to be a model for his painting. I needed a job so I accepted his offer and earned a little money. We became close. He told me I was a source of his inspiration. He said that not only was I physically attractive, I also showed an inner beauty. I was gentle but also strong." Matsumi smiled.

Twinkling stars filled her eyes when she talked about Takeda. Her lips curved into a smile and she looked very happy. Her voice filled with affection when she mentioned his name. Was this love? Father often mentioned Matsumi with the same soulful emotion.

It was painful for me to learn that Father's love turned out to be one-sided. Okasan did not feel the same as he did. Love and longing, which are beautiful emotions, make one lonely and sad when one experiences them alone.

To love and long alone was to be miserable.

It was no longer a surprise that Father died lonely.

Matsumi resumed her story. "Takeda lived by himself. He was twenty-seven years old. He had been married but didn't have any children. His wife left him during the war. She was very greedy and only saw him as a street painter who could not support her. His house was destroyed and his art gallery burned to ashes. The war made him poor. He had to start again with nothing.

"Several weeks after we met, he asked me to live with him. I was confused, doubtful, and scared. I didn't want to make the same mistake. Sujono had given me a bitter lesson and I didn't want to use Takeda for a refuge. I refused his offer and told him of my dark past. I was not ready to open my heart for another man. I only wanted to work so I could save money and return to Indonesia to find you, Kaguya. Men disgusted me. I didn't believe in love."

The old woman, who still looked beautiful, paused before continuing. "Takeda was different. He did not offer me castles in the sky, only gave me comfort. I felt at peace with him. He said, 'Are you ready to live with me in hardship? I won't promise you luxuries, but I won't let you suffer. Come and trust me. Depend on me. I'll give you all I own although I don't have anything except for myself, and all that I am is yours.' Now, that was lovely, wasn't it? Also very reassuring."

I was overwhelmed. Those words were indeed lovely and reassuring. I felt as though I was listening to the sound of birds chirping in the morning, melodious and cheerful. A cool morning breeze caressed my skin, gently and loving. Those words sounded like a *gamelan* orchestra, enchanting and lulling. No wonder Okasan fell in love.

"Takeda didn't talk a lot about his feelings but he gave me all his attention and love. This already said a lot about what he felt. He told me, *anata wo aishiteru,* I love you, only once, but he often says, 'Matsumi, don't leave me.' He never talks about my past as a geisha, or mentions anything about Sujono. He knows it would hurt me. He always says, 'It's no use to keep looking back because life moves toward the future. And the future is my life with you.' He gave me a future and hope for a life as a respectable woman, devoting himself, his life, time, attention, and love to me.

"He was like an alien who extracted me from the spin of time and pulled me into the center of the earth. Being restless and scared, I had no other choice but to say yes. I wanted a normal, peaceful life. We started a simple life together in a small art shop selling his paintings. He liked using me as his model but he never sold any of those paintings. He always said I was his alone. He wouldn't allow anyone to own me, not even in a painting."

I listened to Okasan's story in amazement. It was a touching love story. No wonder Okasan no longer had a place in her heart for my father's love.

"We were very happy and many people liked Takeda's paintings. He often painted nature's beauty, the fog over the Sagano bamboo forest at Arashimaya, or red maple leaves in autumn. All his paintings were as if alive and real. We saved and bought this ryokan to rent out rooms.

"Takeda knew I had a daughter in Indonesia. He did not mind if I looked for her and brought her home. After the country began rebuilding and we had a little money, I traveled to Indonesia twice to look for you. I went to the Hok An Kiong Temple, but Mama Nio, the old lady I entrusted you to, had died. The woman who replaced her knew nothing about you, except that your father had taken you with him. Tuan Tan was no longer there, either. The new caretaker told me that he had gone home to China for good.

"Kembang Jepun had changed. There were no longer entertainment clubs. Instead, there were Chinese shops. I looked for Sujono at Babah Oen's, but the Chinese merchant had also died. His son who succeeded his business told me that Sujono was fired for stealing money.

"I also went to the house I used to live in, hoping your father had taken you there, but the house was locked, unoccupied, and abandoned. Maybe that's when you stayed with his family. I was desperate not knowing where you were. I never knew where your father lived other than with his wife. He moved around a lot.

"I heard from the news that many people, soldiers and civilians alike, had been reported missing. I kept looking for you and followed the news about missing people in the newspaper but I could not find any traces of you. I thought you both had died and I could not forgive myself. I punished myself by mourning endlessly.

"Until finally Takeda said he wanted a child from me. But," Okasan suddenly paused. I quietly waited for her to continue, but she never finished her sentence. After a moment of silence, she continued with her story.

"Takeda said, 'I want to have a child.' We were lying under a warm futon. He hugged me, put my head on his arm, and kissed my hair.

"He whispered, 'Every man wants to have a child from the woman he loves. I always wonder if you really love me. I'm afraid you will leave me.'

"I answered, 'I love you. Do you love me too?' Takeda was not good at expressing his emotions, but every time he tried, he touched me. I actually did not understand love. After I left Indonesia, I didn't want to ever fall in love again. To me, love was very cruel. I didn't know if what I felt for

Takeda was love, compassion, or a passing infatuation. I only knew I was happy.

"Why do men always demand their women to have a child? Was it to secure love, or was a child a symbol of virility, proof that their sperm was capable of fertilizing a woman? This makes children only the product of lovemaking, and turns sex into a machine that produces pans or an oven to bake cakes.

"I had slept with many men since I was a teenager, and earned every cent I was paid. Making love was my job, and I was dependent on it. I knew every inch of a man's body, from head to toe, because I had massaged, caressed, kissed, sucked, and licked it. Not a single inch had escaped my fingers, my lips, my nose, and my tongue.

"I knew a lot about men. I could satisfy them.

"When they were happy, I received money. They became addicted and when they returned for more there was money again for me.

"How could I not know every part of a man's body? I saw sex as a beautiful art that served as a means to money. It was an art to completely satisfy a man, an art that filled my pockets. I never thought of having a child. I felt I lived in paradise.

"But I was wrong. Sex had no meaning with Sujono. He had brutal demands and I had to spend my savings living with him. There was nothing beautiful about our relationship. It was hell.

"Maybe hell is heaven and heaven is hell for Life. There's no difference between them. I had experienced both. What more did I need to go through? Life treated my fate as if He was turning *yakiniku*. Life decided if the meat should be served rare, well done, or even burned. And so Life turned me like a piece of meat, into a prostitute, Tjoa Kim Hwa, Matsumi, whatever suited Him.

"But I needn't have been disappointed or happy, tortured or amused. Everything could change. Everything is temporary, just part of a process. Time moves on, but everything that appears takes its course and then is gone. It's always like that.

"But about Takeda. I can't say anything bad about him. He came into my life unexpectedly, our closeness developed naturally, and I wanted to keep what I had with him. Although I knew some day things would change, I devoted my life to him and resigned myself to the possibility that one day my hopes would be turned into broken branches or fallen leaves.

"I needed to dream. I needed a life. I hoped I needed to love. I needed to live a dream about hope and love. You're alive when you're able to dream.

"Our life was simple; we painted and made love. Making love? How did I make love with Takeda?

"My relationship with him is different from those I've had with other men, including Sujono. I didn't sleep with Takeda because I wanted his money. I knew he was poor. He was a painter who was starting over because the war had taken everything. I was penniless myself. I built my life with him on the canvases. We painted our dreams using the sky, clouds, twigs, and petals of flowers. We poured our souls into every painting. We did not need words, only strokes of color that we applied to the canvas and exhaled with our breath. We were poor but happy.

"Takeda liked to paint on my body. He played with colors, applying them to my skin from head to toe. He stroked my back, shoulders, chest, and thighs with his brushes. It made me happy and turned my soul into a colorful rainbow.

"I did not need sexual fulfillment with Takeda like I did when I was crazy about Sujono. Takeda wasn't a great lover. He rarely kissed me, and when he did, and he always did it quickly, while I wanted to have a longer, deeper, and more affectionate kiss. I was left panting, wanting more. Takeda wasn't a marathon runner. He always had a late start and stopped midway; out of breath and trembling, he was not able to sustain his passion. We never reached yonaki together.

"Takeda startled me when we made love for the first time. Lying besides me, he suddenly climbed on top of me. He did not touch, caress, or kiss me first. I was not ready. While as a geisha I did not need any connection with the man I slept with, it was different now. Sujono had made me dislike sex.

"When I screamed and turned away, Takeda pressed my back with his hand. 'I won't force you,' he said. 'I'll wait until you're ready.'

"I was deeply touched, and also shocked when I realized I had not felt anything hard between my thighs when he was lying on me. I was a woman who knew a lot about men, but I did not understand this man. I didn't know what I felt. I was overwhelmed with disappointment without understanding the cause. I didn't know how and why I could be disappointed.

"When it happened the second time, I wanted to surrender to him. I didn't know why and what I did it for. The desire came suddenly, not because of passion but because I cherished him more everyday.

"I did not do anything when he lay me on the floor, just like when I had my mizuage. He lay on top of me and I felt his skin: cold, moist, and soft. He pressed his cheek on mine so I could hear his breath blowing gently on my ear. I moved my arms to embrace him. I really loved him.

"But when he tried penetrating me, he became overexcited. Then it was finished. Done.

"After that he whispered, '*Anata wo aishiteru.*'

"I was shocked, not only because of the simple way we had made love, but also because he had expressed his feelings. No man had ever said he loved me after being with me. What Takeda said was very beautiful, more beautiful than the art of lovemaking I had learned. I was satisfied, much more than after serving any other man in bed.

"We did it for the second time, and he said, 'I'm scared I won't be able to satisfy you. I'm not strong.' He said that only once, just like he said 'I love you,' only once. He was like other men who nurtured their pride, and refused to admit a weakness. It did not matter to me. I had another kind of fulfillment.

"I enjoyed scrubbing his back in the ofuro, not as something I was required to do like when I was a geisha who had to serve men. I did not have to finish with making love either. I did it because I loved him more every day.

"I was happy when massaging him, a real massage, not a seduction. I massaged his lower stomach, the soles of his feet, and the points between the big and long toes. I did this every night, for one or two hours before going to sleep. It was the geisha's secret therapy to strengthen a man's virility. I had learned it from Yuriko-san.

"I continued doing it for years.

"I asked Takeda, 'How does it feel?'

"He always gave my question back to me. 'I don't know. It's you who feels it, isn't it? What do you feel?'

"I told him, 'It's getting better.'

"Actually, he was not getting any better but I was clever at controlling the game. I guided him patiently and didn't care about my own arousal. The most important to me was to devote my life to him. Our togetherness meant more than anything else.

"I came to understand his ex-wife left him not only because his house and gallery had been destroyed and he didn't have anything left. He also had many weaknesses. Takeda is a very ordinary person. He has a hard time expressing his feelings and keeps disappointments to himself for a long time. He is not good at solving problems; he ignores them and lets them accumulate. He also covered his weaknesses by increasing his demands; he asked for more attention, more understanding, more dreams, and more love.

"I accepted his weaknesses. The more I knew of them, the more I held him dear. I cared about him with all my deepest, genuine feelings. All I wanted was just to give, and that desire became stronger everyday.

"Isn't that how life should be? Nothing is perfect. Life has crevices and gaps. There are always blemishes and mistakes. When people only seek victory, there are wars, and we don't get anything from wars but vengeance and destruction. Moreover, I had labored enough—it was better to accept weakness than search for perfection. Didn't life create everything in pairs? So I did it to fill in the gaps and cover the crevices. This is what I wanted to do with Takeda's longing for a child. I wanted to fulfill it."

Okasan was quiet again. It felt as if she had drowned in her own world, talking to her heart in Japanese. I didn't insist she speak in a language I understood. After a while, she continued her story.

"One day a young girl that worked in a shop next to our gallery gave birth to a son. His father didn't have a steady job and ran away so we decided to adopt the boy as our child although we were old enough to be his grandparents. We named him Higashi. Our life felt more complete and cheerful, filled with his cries, laughter, and babbling."

Okasan took another pause. I felt she was hiding a part of her life she had not told me about. But again I did not force her to tell me. I knew that in everyone's life certain things remained private. Okasan had a gate she kept locked and only she was allowed to go inside.

"It hurt very much to watch Higashi grow up. I always remembered you, Kaguya. I thought about the unfairness of life. Here I was bringing up someone else's child, while I did not know the whereabouts of my own child. While I gave Higashi abundant love and affection, my daughter needed care and love." Okasan's eyes filled with tears.

"Kaguya, you're entitled to hate me."

I bit my lip very hard. I was deeply touched and hurt at the same time. If I were honest, it was not hate that I felt, but disappointment. I did not know why. Was I disappointed in my life, or in my past?

"Okasan, please. Doesn't life always move forward? Despite the obstacles, we have overcome our past. It would be better to talk about something that would make us feel better. Let's talk about the future, our dreams and hopes, about Maya and Higashi," I said faintly. It sounded trite and sentimental, but it was the only thing I could say.

Life does move forward, but the past remains. To forget does not mean to destroy.

"Yes, time goes by so quickly, Kaguya. It flies. The pages of our lives get turned so fast. All of a sudden Higashi has grown up. Seeing him always hurts me. He was never out of my sight, but you always lived in my heart. I never stopped mentioning you in my prayers. I never stopped longing for you. Do you understand, Kaguya?"

Okasan's gentle words penetrated my skin, entered into my bloodstream. It felt soothing. Is this what I had longed for all these years?

I nodded.

Nothing on earth can sever the love connection between a mother and her child.

"Since Higashi liked to follow Takeda around, he came to like painting, too. Once he had the opportunity to visit Surabaya and returned with many paintings of the city. Most of the objects he painted were sections of Kembang Jepun in the morning, during the day, at night and even dawn, when it was empty and quiet. Kembang Jepun is an exotic place whether it is quiet or busy. My heart quivered when I saw the paintings. It was as if I looked at a display of my past. While the area had changed a lot, not everything I used to know was gone.

"Higashi also told me about Maya, the girl he had met in Surabya. He had fallen in love and wanted to marry her and take her to Kyoto. He asked me to ask for Maya's hand for him. What a coincidence," Okasan mumbled.

"I was surprised when I found out that Maya lived in what used to be my house, and even more surprised to hear it was now an orphanage. I kept wondering, who is Maya that she can live there? Ah, what a small world. I never expected to find you at my own house. Everything has gone full circle. You were born in that house and in the end, I found you there." Okasan's voice broke. Tears streamed down her face and she was overcome by her emotions.

"Yes, it is such a small world, and time goes by very fast," I replied in a raspy voice.

*****

I spent two weeks in Kyoto. During that time Okasan and I became very close. We not only developed a mother and daughter bond, we also became friends. We talked about many things. I told her about the orphanage while she talked about Takeda's paintings and gallery, their ryokan and bonsai. Our stories flowed freely. And like water flows from the spring into the river and empties into the sea, our stories emptied into the deepest part of our hearts.

Okasan taught me about ikebana and bonsai, and I cooked Indonesian dishes for her. She played the shamisen for me and I took her arm when we walked together. We laughed and cried together, and shared our feelings about love, care, and desire. The two weeks redeemed the bitter decades. A beautiful short time is very meaningful, where a long time filled with anger feels empty.

My heart overflowed with warmth when the two people dearest to me, Okasan and Maya, hugged me at the Narita Airport before I returned to Surabaya.

"Mother, I'll come often to Surabaya to see you. I'll always miss you," Maya said, affectionately.

"Kaguya, come back to Kyoto and visit me. I'll always long for you," Okasan said, softly.

Two different people said two different things, but both conveyed the same message— love, the love of a daughter for her mother and love of a mother for her daughter. It was so beautiful and sweet.

That is how love is supposed to be. The love between a mother and her child is the most beautiful and sweetest experience on earth; it is a love that rises from the heart.

It is happiness.

Epilogue

Surabaya, February 2004

After spending the day tidying up her bedroom, Lestari took out a package and unwrapped it carefully. She had wanted to do this since returning from Kyoto last year, but the orphanage had taken so much of her time as now she ran it alone. The package contained a painting.

Takeda had given her the painting when she was going to return to Surabaya. He took her and Matsumi to his gallery. He said he had a special gift for her.

In the gallery, Lestari saw many paintings in different sizes. Every one of them showed Takeda's mastery of fine strokes and composition of natural colors. Most of his paintings were landscapes, flowers, and trees. They looked as if they were real.

In a corner of the gallery, a canvas was covered with a piece of cloth. The pungent smell of paint still hung in the air.

Translated by Okasan, Takeda said, "I painted this specially for you, Kaguya. I just finished it this week. I rushed, so it might not be perfect. I want you to take this to Surabaya."

Lestari bowed deeply. "Takeda-san, *arigato gozaimasu, terima kasih*, thank you."

"Open and have a look. I hope you'll like it."

Lestari carefully removed the cloth that covered the canvas. As the painting appeared, she caught her breath. She also heard Matsumi gasp in surprise. They both looked in astonishment at the picture of the woman on the canvas. She wore a bright orange kimono and knelt, providing the painter with a side view. Her kimono collar plunged so her perfect ivory-skinned shoulder showed. Her beautiful face had a somber expression and her pretty eyes were filled with tears. Yet she radiated a loveliness that resided in hope and a genuine surrender to love.

The woman sat under a dormant cherry tree. In the background was a full sun of orange with red hues.

She was breathtaking.

"That's how Matsumi looked when we first met at a shrine. She was so lovely with her gloomy face, exquisite in her vulnerability and alluring in her sadness. I fell in love with her at first sight. Kaguya, a poet once said one needs a long time to forget love, but only seconds to fall in love. That's what happened to me.

"Matsumi drove me crazy. She was like a fairy whose breath warmed my chest, and then the warmth spread throughout my whole body. She was the most beautiful woman I'd ever seen. She made me feel drunk; I felt as if I had swallowed many cups of sake. But it was a delightful intoxication. I always felt infatuated whenever I saw her.

"I knew immediately that she was the woman who would bring perfect happiness in my life. She would make me complete and always stand by me. Her sadness made me want to make her happy. Her gloom made me want to make her laugh. Her fragility made me want to become someone she could depend on. I was willing to be anything for Matsumi and do anything for her."

Lestari was overwhelmed listening to Takeda. His words were so affectionate and full of love. She never thought she'd hear such romantic words from a man as old as Takeda. Actually, she had never heard words of love; practically none had ever reached her ears.

If there had been any, it was her father's mumbling of his deep longing for Matsumi. It was only a painful yearning—there were wounds in there. He was like a man trying to net the sun.

It was in vain, useless.

Her father's love was very different from what she heard from Takeda. His words were full of assurance. He spoke of love that did not demand but instead offered his entire self to make Matsumi happy.

Lestari saw Matsumi softly touch the back of Takeda's hand. No words were necessary to confirm that Matsumi was truly happy.

Feeling their love, Lestari held her breath; it is never too late for love.

"Matsumi is always beautiful and perfect in my heart and mind. She gives me happiness and makes my dreams real."

Now Lestari understood how Matsumi became the most popular geisha in Kyoto when she was young and why men loved her so much. There was Major General Kobayashi, who took her to Indonesia; Sujono, her father, a man of Matsumi's past who was crazy about her and loved her selfishly; and now Takeda, the man who gave her comfort and made her enjoy her days peacefully. Perhaps many other men secretly admired her because Matsumi made them adore her and made it difficult for them to forget her.

She was indeed a beautiful woman.

"I haven't given the painting a title. I'll let Kaguya do that since it's for her," Takeda said.

"Me? Give a title to this painting?" Lestari stammered. She was quiet, as if hypnotized by the strength of their love.

"*Haik*, yes. I'm asking you to title this painting of Matsumi."

Lestari turned thoughtful. She was confused and delighted. Takeda's request had moved her.

"What about *The Lady from Kembang Jepun*?"

"The Lady from Kembang Jepun," Takeda and Matsumi exclaimed together.

Notes

Prologue
Reog Ponorogo: Javanese traditional dance.
Okasan: Japanese for mother.

Part 1
Mas: Literally meaning "elder brother," a Javanese term of
     address to an older male. Also used to refer to a younger
     male to show respect.
Priyayis: Javanese elite.
Jamu: Traditional herbal potion sold in bottles and carried
     on the backs of women peddlers in a plaited bamboo
     basket.
Klobot: Cigarette wrapped in dried cornhusk, or *klobot.*
Parikan: Javanese poetic form consisting of two sentences.
Yu: Abbreviation of *mbakyu,* meaning "elder sister," a
     Javanese term of address to an older female. Like Mas
     for males, it is also used to refer to a younger female to

show respect. Yu is normally used among the working class.

Kebaya: Long-sleeved blouse closed in the front with pins.

Kain: Rectangular piece of batik cloth used as a wrap-around skirt.

Batik: Javanese traditional patterned cloth dyed with wax.

Ndhuk: Address for young girl.

Maghrib: Muslim evening praying time, just after sunset.

Kang: Used to call for brother or husband.

Besar: Month in the Javanese lunar calendar, considered a good time to hold significant life events, like a wedding.

Kampung: Javanese for village.

Bapak, or *Pak*: Meaning "Father." *Pak* is the abbreviation and both are respectful terms of address, like "sir."

PETA: Stands for Pembela Tanah Air, Defenders of the Homeland, the Indonesian volunteer army established by the Japanese during their occupation of the country.

Hinomaru: The Rising Sun.

Durna: A character in the Mahabharata, assimilated into the traditional Javanese culture usually associated with craftiness.

Part 2

Spaanche matten: Dutch currency of the time.

Kapitan: Captain.

Ofuro: Steep-sided wooden bathtub.

Kimono: Japanese robe worn by men and women.

Obi: Sash belt worn with kimono.

Shamisen: Traditional three-stringed Japanese musical instrument.

Yukata: A light cotton kimono, normally worn in the summer or for the bath.

Fuse: Japanese, meaning an order to lie prone.

Hajime: Japanese, meaning an order to start.

Atsumare: Japanese, meaning an order to assemble.

Lampion: A small oil lamp.

Kanji: Japanese alphabet.

Part 3

Warung: Small, family-owned business, usually a coffee stand built of bamboo mats.

Part 4

Soekarno and Hatta: Indonesia's first president and vice president.

Subuh: Muslim evening praying time, just before dawn.

Part 5

Kuntilanak: A pale-skinned female ghost with long hair and dressed in white, often depicted with a hole in her back covered by the hair. She died in childbirth and goes around stealing babies.

Gamelan: A traditional Javanese ensemble.

Yakiniku: Japanese dish of bite-sized meat and vegetables cooked on a griddle heated with charcoal; also known as Japanese barbeque.

About the Author

Lan Fang was born in Banjarmasin, Kalimantan, Indonesia on March 5, 1970, and passed away on December 25, 2011. She was the oldest daughter in the Gautama family of business people.

Despite a law degree from the University of Surabaya, Lan Fang chose to pursue a writing career. Her novel, *Lelakon,* won the Khatulistiwa Award in 2008. Her short stories have appeared in *20 Cerpen Terbaik Indonesia* as a part of the Anugerah Sastra Pena Kencana (Pena Kencana Literary Awards) in 2008 and 2009.

In 2009, the newspaper *Kompas* published Lan Fang's "Ciuman di bawah Hujan" as a serial and in 2010 Gramedia Pustaka Utama published the story as a novel under the same title. Other books by Lan Fang from the same publisher include: *Reinkarnasi* (2003), *Pai Yin* (2004), *Kembang Gunung Purei* (2005), *Laki-Laki yang Salah* (2006), *Yang Liu* (2006), *Perempuan Kembang Jepun* (2006; reprinted 2012), *Kota Tanpa Kelamin* (2007), and *Lelakon* (2007).

Lan Fang is known in Indonesia as an accomplished writer, and also a philanthropist with deep concern for social welfare. Her beliefs are shown in her writing, as well as through her volunteer work as a mentor for several writing workshops in schools.

Unfortunately, this prolific writer's life was cut short. Lan Fang passed away at the age of forty-one while being treated for liver cancer in Singapore. Her untimely death is a great loss to the Indonesian literary community, and to every reader who appreciates evocative, truthful writing of the heart.

While *Perempuan Kembang Jepun* was being prepared for its first edition in 2006, Lan Fang visited the publisher's offices and asked that the following poem be included.

I learned to talk to silence. Because loneliness has
befriended me.
Death kissed me, so the red of the peacock flowers
are not bright enough to brighten my eyes,
although the light hasn't ended, and the claws of chaos
still scratch and hurt.
"If only every being that has breath could thank
their faults," so you said.
"You're good to me, respect me, and love me,
in the past, now, and hopefully forever. I could die
without you,"
I replied to the fog.
Because you are the quakes of the storming chaos.

POTIONS AND PAPER CRANES

Like Jesus shouting, "*Eli, Eli, lama sabakhtani,*" and
the blood
trickling down from His side.
What should I shout if the lingering loneliness has
stabbed my tongue,
except to moan to the reverie, "My pitch is off key,
my voice is limping. This is not the song I want.
I'm not Siddhartha or Kemala, neither Jesus nor
Mary Magdalena."
Like magic, the reverie turned my chaos into harmony.
It may be
offkey, it may be limping, but there is peace after the
storm.
It is the flower that teaches me to sip a cup of hot
chocolate
slowly so I could enjoy it more!

Surabaya, 22.08.2006, 23.32 pm
Pro:…??
Is going straight too difficult for you?

More Storytellers from Dalang Publishing

Only a Girl
Lian Gouw

Three generations of Chinese women struggle for identity against a political backdrop of the World Depression, World War II, and the Indonesian Revolution. Nanna, the matriarch of the family, strives to preserve the family's traditional Chinese values while her children are eager to assimilate into Dutch colonial society. Carolien, Nanna's youngest daughter, is fixated on the advantages to be gained by adopting a western lifestyle. Jenny's western upbringing puts her at a disadvantage in the newly independent Indonesian state where Dutch culture is no longer revered. The unique ways in which Nanna, Carolien and Jenny face their own challenges reveal the complex tale of Chinese society in Indonesia between 1930 and 1952.

Price: $17.95
Paperback: 298 pages
ISBN: 978-0-9836273-7-1

My Name is Mata Hari
Remy Sylado
English rendition by Dewi Anggraeni

My Name is Mata Hari tells the story of the infamous dancer and courtesan who began as Margaretha Geertruida Zelle, a young Dutch woman who married the older Rudolph MacLeod, a military officer, and traveled with him to the Dutch East Indies. Claiming her mother's Javanese ancestry, she changed her name to Mata Hari, Malay for "eye of the day."

Mata Hari danced on stages across Europe and the Middle East, and took many high-ranking military and government officials as her lovers. At the end of a tumultuous life, convicted for espionage during the First World War yet sustained by her pride, she said, "I am a genuine courtesan. And I am a dancer in the true sense."

Price: $17.95
Paperback: 334 pages
ISBN: 978-0-9836273-0-2

Dalang Publishing books are available from our website www.dalangpublishing.com, Amazon, Barnes & Noble, and IndieBound bookstores.